Leo

Dog of the Sea

Alison Hart
Illustrated by Michael G. Montgomery

PEACHTREE
PUBLISHERS

Published by
PEACHTREE PUBLISHERS
1700 Chattahoochee Avenue
Atlanta, Georgia 30318-2112
www.peachtree-online.com

Edited by Kathy Landwehr
Map and illustrations on pages 149, 157, and 163 by Adela Pons
Cover design by Nicola Simmonds Carmack
Interior design and composition by Melanie McMahon Ives

Cover illustration rendered in oil on canvas board; interior illustrations in pencil.

Printed in February 2017 in the United States of America by LSC Communications in Harrisonburg, Virginia
10 9 8 7 6 5 4 3 2 1
First Edition

Library of Congress Cataloging-in-Publication Data
Names: Hart, Alison, 1950- author. | Montgomery, Michael, 1952- illustrator.
Title: Leo, dog of the sea / written by Alison Hart ; illustrated by Michael
    G. Montgomery.
Description: Atlanta, GA : Peachtree Publishers, [2017] | Summary: "Leo is a
    hardened old sea dog who knows not to trust anyone but himself after three
    ocean voyages. But when he sets sail with Magellan on a journey to find a
    westward route to the Spice Islands, he develops new friendships as they
    experience hunger and thirst, storms and doldrums, and mutinies and
    hostile, violent encounters. Will they ever find safe passage?"— Provided
    by publisher.
Identifiers: LCCN 2016017196 | ISBN 9781561459643
Subjects: LCSH: Dogs—Juvenile fiction. | Magellan, Ferdinand, d.
    1521—Juvenile fiction. | CYAC: Dogs—Fiction. | Magellan, Ferdinand, d.
    1521—Fiction. | Explorers—Fiction. | Discoveries in geography—Fiction.
    | Voyages around the world—Fiction. | Sea stories.
Classification: LCC PZ10.3.H247 Le 2017 | DDC [Fic]—dc23 LC record available at
    https://lccn.loc.gov/2016017196

To all the brave explorers who overcame adversity
to discover new cultures and lands

—A. H.

CONTENTS

Leo's Journey with Magellan

ATLANTIC
OCEAN

PACIFIC
OCEAN

Sanlúcar de Barrameda

Canary Islands

Bahía Santa Lucía

Cape Desire

Port Saint Julian

Strait of Magellan

Homonhon

Mactan
Cebu

Limasawa

PACIFIC
OCEAN

Isla de los Ladrones

Spice Islands

INDIAN
OCEAN

CHAPTER 1

Sanlúcar de Barrameda, Spain

August 1519

R*ato!"* a gruff voice hollers as a toe nudges my ribs. Steward points to a dark corner. A furry ball, its naked tail twitching, scurries along the ship's wall. A chunk of bread is clamped in its mouth.

I jump from my sunny spot on deck. Steward is in charge of supplies, so he is important on the ship, and I try to obey. He uses chalk to mark and count casks and bundles as they are being brought onboard. After they are stored below, he alone has the keys, which jingle on a cord around his fat waist.

He jerks his thumb toward the rat, and I race after it. It darts around ropes and barrels, more nimble than I—no longer a pup. My claws rake the deck as I scuttle around a coil of rope.

I leap over a burlap sack. Too late: the rat slips through a hole in the wood flooring, and I bark in frustration.

A sailor stumbles over me. The crew is loading the last of the supplies. Steward shouts at the men, directing them this way and that. I duck out of their way, knowing the importance of their task. Wine, chickpeas, rice, honey, and cheese are necessary to feed the men at sea during our long journey. The supplies also act as ballast, packed carefully in the hull to keep the ship balanced.

Raising my muzzle, I breathe deeply. This is my fourth voyage, and I now have a sailor's nose. The breezes from the Ocean Sea are salty; the breezes from the Guadalquivir River are muddy. My nose also picks up the smell of chickens and pigs. They're already stashed below in cages and pens. Then I

smell *bizcocho,* the hard biscuits the crew is forced to eat when there are no fresh foods. The wheaty odor wafts from one of the bags a sailor is hauling from a smaller boat below. The rats will quickly find them, so I must keep alert.

Voices holler and sing on deck and above in the rigging. As on most voyages, the crew members of the *Trinidad* are from many countries. I don't understand their words, but that's fine with me. For truth, I stay away from humans and their sunbaked, sweaty skin.

As a pup, my home was the streets of Seville, Spain. I survived by eating garbage tossed out doors and windows. I stumbled onto my first ship by chance, following the scent of cod. I found a job killing rats and mice, and since then, my home has been different carracks and caravels. Stewards may holler at me. Sailors may curse me. But the only master I serve is the ship.

Five weeks ago, the *Trinidad* departed Seville with me onboard. Before the ship left, I explored it from bow to stern. My nose told me the contents of each bundle and crate. My inspection told me that the ship was being loaded with ample supplies and a strong crew. All good signs, so I decided it would be my next home. Today we are docked before heading to sea, and I sense an anxious energy as well as a rise in activity, which means we will soon set sail.

Leaving the sailors to their loading, I continue my exploration. For a long journey, the *Trinidad* must be shipshape. I check the caulker, who is tarring the mast. Already the hull, deck, and riggings are black with pitch to help make them watertight.

Then I trot back to the stern, jump up to the quarterdeck, and check on the carpenter, who is nailing a loose board. Below us is the captain general's cabin. I have heard him called Magellan, but as yet I have not seen him.

On the forecastle, which is at the bow end of the ship, Hernando the barber is pulling a sailor's tooth. He grunts and wrestles, finally yelling "aha!" when he pulls out a bloody mess. Like Steward, Hernando is also important on the ship. He has charge over body, mind, and teeth of all the crew. I avoid him and his pliers at all costs.

Catching the scent of cooking food, I detour to the crackling fire in the cookstove on the main deck. An apprentice sailor has several cod laced on a spit. When he turns his back, I grab the stick from the flame. With sharp teeth I rip off one blackened fish. It burns my tongue, but, holding it tightly, I jump though the open hatch to the gun deck. It is lined with cannons. Gunners are cleaning weapons, and several pages, the youngest crew members, are scrubbing the wood flooring. I skirt them and climb down the ladder into the dank hold, which smells of mice, mold, and feathers. Dark-skinned sailors sing as they secure the last of the supplies.

I wiggle between the barrels, placed on their sides, which follow the curve of the ship's hull. There is a narrow tunnel between them, and, carrying the cod, I worm my way to my sleeping nest, which is a space between the fragrant barrels of salted tuna and pork.

Suddenly my hackles rise. A boy is curled in my nest. His cheeks are sunken. His eyes and mop of hair are as black as his dirty skin. He licks his lips when he sees the cod sticking from my mouth. I growl a warning.

He swallows hard, and I sense his fear. His bare feet are pocked with sores. His tunic barely covers his legs. Slowly he curls into himself as if warding off an attack. I drop the cod, then turn and crawl from the tunnel.

Why am I willing to give my meal to this vermin, this human *bicho?* Perhaps because I remember when I was a pup and my stomach was always empty.

Hopping up the wooden ladder to the main deck, I trot to the cookfire, using the shadows cast by the masts and rigging overhead to stay out of sight. I pass the scribe Pigafetta, a strange figure on the ship. He wears a velvet overgown, silk hose, and a wide-brimmed hat, not the ragged trousers and tunics of the sailors. He sits on a crate, scratching notes onto parchment with a pen. As I pass, he makes friendly clucking noises like a chicken and reaches to pat me. I dodge his fingers.

The sailors are clustered around the cookfire, catching a last bite before we set sail. If I am patient, one may drop a crumb.

"In the Caribbean, we picked fruits dripping with sweet juice," a scrawny man says as he shovels handfuls of rice into his mouth. "Sailed in water as blue as the sky. And romanced women with copper-colored skin."

"And where will *this* voyage lead us, Diego?" a page asks him. The young pages are the least seaworthy and most frightened of what lies ahead.

"The captain general has not been clear," a hefty sailor named Vasco replies. The others call him *la Bestia*—Beast—because he is so strong.

"We'll make a stop at the Moluccas, the Spice Islands, for sure," Diego says. "Thus we and the four ships sailing with us are called the Armada de Molucca."

"We're sailing with an armada of four other ships?" asks Dias, a sailor with a dirty beard. "When I signed on, the master-at-arms did not tell me this."

"Aye." Beast nods knowingly. "The *San Antonio, Concepción, Victoria,* and *Santiago.* But make no mistake, the captain general of the *Trinidad* leads them all to our destination."

"How long is the journey, do you think?" Dias asks.

"Who knows? Magellan has ordered provisions for a year." Diego smiles mysteriously as he leans forward. "For truth, I have heard whispers that this voyage is guaranteed to be like no other."

Excited murmurs travel from sailor to sailor. My ears prick.

For a moment I forget about my empty belly. The air seems to tingle. My whiskers vibrate.

Jumping from the shadows, I place my paws on the railing. The bowsprit points like an arrow toward the horizon. Waves crash against the bow below me.

Above me in the foremast, I hear sailors call to each other.

The strong wind flaps my ears. I stare out at the vast, churning sea—and wonder at the adventures ahead.

CHAPTER 2

Sanlúcar de Barrameda, Spain

September–November 1519

A hearty bellow makes me turn from the ocean. "All hands at attention for Captain General Ferdinand Magellan!"

The sailors and pages pop to their feet and rub rice-sticky palms against their trousers. Others swing down from the rigging above. Finally the crew stands in two ragged lines, shoulders back. They are a strong but seedy bunch.

Dropping behind a pair of hairy legs, I peer at our leader, Magellan. He struts between the lines, nodding as he inspects each sailor. He wears a fur-trimmed overgown and a round hat. Beside him walk the *Trinidad*'s pilots and behind him is Enrique, Magellan's brown-skinned servant.

Another man inspects the seamen from behind the line. Scowling, he prods each sailor with the hilt of his sword, ordering them to "stand tall" and "look lively for the captain general." As he approaches me, his eyebrows raise.

"*Cao sujo*," he says in Portuguese. "Dirty mongrel, stay out of my sight." He raises his sword. "Or you will find yourself skewered like a pig on a spit."

I scuttle away to hide among the ropes and tarps. The fierce-eyed officer joins Magellan as they climb to the quarterdeck.

"I introduce Gonzalo Gomez de Espinosa, master-at-arms." Magellan points to him. "He will carry out my orders and assure that the laws of Spain and navigation are obeyed."

Crouching, I stare at Espinosa. I sense this man will cause problems for me and the ship.

Bowing his head, Magellan leads the crew in prayer. Then the two pilots step forward and shout orders.

"Raise the anchor!" one of the pilots yells, and a score of sailors hauls the thick hemp rope. A handful of men turns the capstan, which groans as the rope winds around it and the anchor is raised.

"Ease the foresail!" the other pilot hollers. "Hoist the yards!"

Sailors rush in all directions. Several use the rope shrouds as ladders to climb to the top of the masts. Sails catch the wind as they are unfurled. The ship begins to sway. Soon I will need sturdy sea legs.

I have witnessed setting sail many times, so I go below, curious to see if the boy is still in my nest. I didn't see him among the pages and apprentice sailors who are scurrying like cockroaches on the main deck. If he's still hidden, it must mean that he is a stowaway. Perhaps the boy is like me and left a hard life on land for a hard life at sea.

The lower deck is empty except for the gunners. I

climb halfway down the ladder and look around the hold. My eyes adjust to the dark and I spy the boy venturing from my tunnel. A full belly has made him bolder. Or perhaps it's the rush of water against the hull. The *Trinidad* is moving into the vast ocean. Thus there is no return for stowaways, reluctant sailors, or sea dogs such as I.

The winds send the *Trinidad* southward to the Canary Islands and then along the coast of Africa. The *San Antonio, Concepción, Victoria,* and *Santiago* bob behind us like ducks. Magellan rules all the ships, using torches, lanterns, and cannon blasts to signal orders from the *Trinidad.*

Each night a *farol* of wood burns on the poop deck. This is so the other ships in our armada can keep sight of the *Trinidad.* Two lights signal a change in the wind. Four lights mean the ships should lower the sails quickly. The cannons are also used to send messages, and their booms can be heard night and day.

One windy night, the stowaway sneaks from the hull to find food. He crouches over the fire, picking scraps from the embers. Espinosa is patrolling, and I know in my bones that something bad will happen.

Should I alert the boy about Espinosa? It is not my duty to keep him safe, but I find myself trotting to the cookfire. Suddenly a shadow passes over me and a gruff voice booms, "What do we have here? A ship's rat?"

I cower, waiting for a boot to find my ribs, but Espinosa is focused on the boy. He grabs the neck of his tunic and lifts him in the air. "Perhaps it needs to be thrown overboard."

For a moment the boy kicks his legs in defiance. But then he gives up and hangs like a sail with no wind.

The sailors pause to stare. They do not care about a filthy stowaway. But they care for Espinosa even less, and a few cast angry looks at him.

Grinning wickedly, Espinosa carries the boy to the railing. I have no feelings for the boy. If he is tossed into the sea, it will make more room for me. But all ships have men like Espinosa who rule with fists. My hatred of these bullies dates back to when I was a pup and received my first blow. Now that anger spills out, and, rushing forward, I sink my teeth into Espinosa's calf.

He bellows, drops the boy, and whirls around to strike me.

The boy and I are gone in a flash through the hatch. Espinosa hurries after us, but the sailors throw ropes in his path and unfurl sails by his head while shouting, "*Perdón,* Master Espinosa. *Perdón!* But the wind is bringing a storm and we must turn leeward away from the gale…"

The boy disappears into the crates. I hide in the weapons cache and wait for the thud of Espinosa's boots, but the wind begins to scream, and the ship lists violently. My bones tell me that the sailors are right: a storm will soon be upon us.

I always know about bad weather before it arrives. My sharp ears pick up the distant crack of thunder. My aging joints ache as the air grows heavy. Now every sense is tingling.

It's not long before the full force of the storm hits us, and the boy and I are forgotten.

For sixty long days, winds, waves, rain, and lightning pummel the five ships, which buck and twist like angry carthorses. The crew is exhausted from nights of no sleep. Espinosa has wisely turned his attention to the weather, and when he sees the boy, he treats him like any other page who must work from dawn to dusk. But sometimes I see the glare in his eyes when he spots me, and I scoot away.

Finally one night after sailors and officers have given up hope, a few stars twinkle in a patch of clear sky. The men cheer and rush to build up the cookfire to dry their clothes and warm some food.

But a flash of lightning on the horizon raises my fur. The storms are not over.

The wind whooshes across the ocean again.

Sailors cross themselves. This storm hits at the break of dawn, plunging the *Trinidad* into darkness.

"All hands! All hands!" the boatswain hollers as the rain pelts us. "Gather the sails!" The ship rears in the swells, and I skitter along the deck.

"All hands aloft!" Magellan orders. "Man top-gallant mast ropes! Steady on!"

Sailors climb the shrouds, disappearing into the gloom. Some cling high to the thrashing masts. Others handle the ropes, their backs braced against the wind.

When a fierce wave douses me, I jump into the hold, but it is wet too, and the men are busy with bilge pumps that suck water from the ship's belly and force it back into the sea.

The crew has formed a bucket line as well, and the boy has joined them. By this time, no one questions why he is onboard as long as he works as hard as they do.

After what seems like forever there is another lull in the foul weather, and I hurry back on deck to gulp fresh air. Several sailors are leaning over the rail, gesturing excitedly. I stick my head between the railings to see what they are speaking of.

"The *squali* have been circling us day and night," Beast says. "Hoping the gale will toss one of us into the sea."

"Sharks." Pigafetta nods as he sketches in his journal. "I have read about the creatures." His wide-brimmed hat is gone, replaced by a soggy velvet one. The hem of his overgown is wet to his knees.

"Diego, when you catch one, I can use the oil from the creature's liver," Hernando says. "It heals sores and sunburn."

Pigafetta is immediately interested. "Tell me of this medicine," he says as he turns a page in his journal.

The sharks flash gray and white in the waves below us. One leaps from the water, mouth wide, as if waiting for me to drop into his jaws.

"They will eat you in an instant, so beware," Diego warns. He and Beast lower a thick rope; at the end is an iron hook baited with cod. "But a small one will be tasty after so many days of dry biscuits."

A shark clamps its sharp teeth around the hook. Diego and Beast slowly haul it up, grunting as it bangs against the hull, fighting them.

High above, thunder rumbles and my hair stands up. The storm is back again!

Diego and Beast give one last hard yank and the shark and the rain hit the deck at the same time. I jump clear of the creature, which flips and twists on the wet wood. Its tail strikes Pigafetta, knocking him over. He scrambles away on all fours like a dog.

From the corner of my eye I spy the boy. His eyes are wide with fear. The ship lists, pitching all of us to the edge. Waves slam onto the deck, and the skinny boy is engulfed. A surge picks him up, drags him to the rail, and pitches him halfway over.

With a mighty leap I grasp the hem of his tunic and hold tightly. The ship tilts in the other direction and he flops on top of me. Together we slide to the mainmast. The boy hugs me with one arm while his other circles the sturdy beam. Frothy waves wash over us, trying to drag us into the sea, and I feel his arm tremble.

Finally the storm weakens. The boy buries his face in my wet fur. "*Gracias*," he whispers before letting me go.

Suddenly the air is filled with a bright light. My whiskers vibrate as I pull away from the boy. It looks

like a plume of fire is rising over the mast, yet the ship is not in flames. The crew stares upwards and begins to cheer.

Pigafetta hoists himself to his feet. "What is this wonder?" he asks.

"A sign that Saint Elmo has saved us from the storms!" Hernando cries out.

"Saint Elmo?" Pigafetta asks as he again writes furiously in his journal.

"The patron saint of mariners." Hernando falls to his knees beside Diego and Beast, who hold up their hands as if praying. The shark lies dead at their feet. I sniff it, wondering how it will taste.

"It is an omen that all will be well," Diego says solemnly.

Just then Magellan appears on the quarterdeck. The strange light seems to play about his head before slowly vanishing. "Our captain general must be holy," the boy whispers after the sky has turned light gray once again.

"Perhaps he is. And you are?" Pigafetta asks.

"Marco." The boy shifts his feet as if suddenly wary. "Polo."

Pigafetta raises one brow. "You named yourself after the great explorer, I presume."

The boy nods. "*Sí*, at the convent I read about his travels."

"Ah, a child who has education." Pigafetta seems impressed with the raggedy *bicho*. The rain has washed the boy, and he is no longer black with grime. Still, his tunic is tattered and clings to his thin frame.

"And I am Antonio Pigafetta of Venice, chronicler of this voyage." He holds up his journal.

"Pleased to meet such a worthy scholar."

"Not as worthy as the ship's dog. Saint Elmo may have saved the *Trinidad*, but the dog saved you, Marco," Pigafetta says. "I was amazed at his heroics during the storm."

"He is brave." Marco smiles shyly at me. "He saved me once before as well. From the master-at-arms, who was about to throw me overboard."

I clean my wet paws, trying not to show interest.

23

Seldom do humans speak about me unless the word *rat* is on their tongues.

"Ah, yes, our ever-vigilant Gonzalo Gomez de Espinosa does enjoy flaunting his authority." Pigafetta nods at me. "Here I thought the dog was only the ship's ratter with no name. Perhaps we should give him one now that he has proven himself. How about Leo—for his lionlike bravery?"

"*Sí.*" Marco reaches to pat me, but I scoot away.

Leo. I will take their name—the sound pleases me. But I will not take their affection or attention, so I trot off.

The *Trinidad* has survived months of storms. Now the cookfires are once again burning. Diego and Beast slice flesh from the shark and I, Leo the Brave, lick my lips at the thought of a delicious meal.

CHAPTER 3

Sailing to the Equator

November 1519

Saint Elmo does not bless the armada for long. The sky grows calm, but so does the wind. The sails do not billow. The five ships bob helplessly, no land in sight.

The fresh food has long since disappeared. The chicken cages are empty. The sun is stifling and the men grow listless from the heat and from hunger.

Steward guards the barrels and bundles so even a sly dog cannot steal a crumb. Espinosa struts on deck, his orders harsh as the men toil under the relentless sun. Hernando tries to cure heatstroke with cool rags and soothe sunburn with shark oil. Diego and Beast fish, but nothing is biting. My belly rumbles since the rats hide in the farthest corners.

During the second week of heat, Espinosa calls the crew together. I prick my ears, wondering what is going on. Has an island been spotted? I am eager to roll in dirt and lap from a stream. As they gather on deck, the sailors murmur excitedly among themselves.

"From this day on, each man receives only four pints of water a day," Espinosa reads from a parchment. Steward is beside him, clutching the keys to the supplies. "He receives a pound and a half of hardtack. Wine is reduced by half."

I can tell from the angry looks that this is not the news the sailors hoped for. "Our throats are parched!" one yells.

"Our stomachs are empty!"

"We need to find land and fresh supplies!"

"First storms, now trapped in equatorial calms!" a new voice chimes in. "It is Magellan's fault that we are traveling this reckless course."

All eyes turn toward the speaker. He is dressed as an officer in a wide-brimmed hat, bright red over-gown with puffy sleeves, silken hose, and leather boots to his knees. A priest, wearing a loose brown robe belted with a leather strap, walks a step behind him.

"If I was in command, the ship would be moving swiftly," the officer continues. "Food and wine would be abundant for all!"

The sailors give a rousing cheer. Even Pigafetta, who stands aloof from the crew, seems heartened by this new officer's words.

Espinosa, though, is speechless. Then he bows. "Welcome to the *Trinidad,* Juan de Cartagena, captain of the *San Antonio,* and Pero Sanchez de la Reina, chaplain of the *San Antonio.* Captain General Magellan is waiting for you. He is in the cabin with the other captains."

One of the mates escorts Cartagena and de la Reina toward the stern.

I had seen the other captains rowing to the

27

Trinidad earlier. But I did not know why. Could it be that we've reached the Spice Islands? Peering between the railings, I search for a hummock of land on the horizon, but the glassy ocean stretches forever.

When the mate opens the door to the cabin, angry voices spill from within. It is the sound of trouble.

Cartagena ushers the priest inside and then announces, "By the orders of King Charles, I will no longer obey your commands, Magellan!" The door shuts quickly behind them.

Espinosa turns his attention back to the crew. "Complainers will be swiftly dealt with." He nods toward the stocks. On other ships, I have seen men held in the hinged boards, their hands and legs locked in as if they were oxen.

"The captain general will not tolerate mutiny or ungodly behavior," Espinosa continues. "From officers or seamen."

When an ominous murmur rises from the crew, I know that the word *mutiny* must mean something bad.

Espinosa draws his sword. Turning, he marches into the captain general's cabin with two other armed men. The air is tense. The sailors are silent as they stare at the closed door. They grumble among themselves about the new orders for reduced food and wine.

Marco stands behind Pigafetta's robes as if he's hiding from the rest. "The other ships' captains, led by Cartagena, are plotting against Captain General Magellan," Pigafetta is saying to the boy in a low voice. For some reason he has taken a liking to the *bicho*. He's even given him a new tunic, which is baggy but clean.

"Why?"

"Magellan is Portuguese. Captain Cartagena, the priests, and the other captains are Spanish. They do not believe Magellan is loyal to Spain, even though he is leading the armada for the Spanish King Charles." He nods toward the cabin. "I fear this meeting will not go well."

Suddenly the door bangs open. "Rebel! This is

mutiny!" Magellan pushes Cartagena from the cabin. "You are my prisoner in the king's name!"

Magellan's words boom through the air like shots. Members of the crew step back or, like me, hasten in other directions. Pigafetta stands his ground and watches as Espinosa and Cristovao grab Cartagena and drag him to the stocks. They force his head and wrists into the slots and lower the wood, locking him in.

"I should sentence you to death for your defiance," Magellan continues as he strides over. The other captains follow him, loudly proclaiming their loyalty. "Instead, I strip you of your command and confine you to the *Victoria*. If your presence darkens my ship again, you will be killed."

Whirling, he raises his arms. "Sound the trumpets!" he orders. "Fire the cannons! Let the other ships know that henceforth *San Antonio*'s captain will be Antonio de Coca, a man of honor."

The gunners light the cannons, which boom loudly. The trumpeter raises his horn. The noise

hurts my ears, and I jump below and wiggle my way to the safety of my nest.

Like me, sailors are loyal only to themselves. Many are forced to go to sea because of debts or poverty. Others are slaves with no choice. Still others are lawless thieves. Thus they only obey if beaten or if it serves them.

I sense that the men hurrying above are angry and restless. Today they might follow the orders of Magellan and his enforcer, Espinosa. Tomorrow they may not. Magellan may be our leader, but his officers and crew are as troublesome as the devious rats and mice that keep me busy.

Shivering, I curl in a ball. Humans turn against each other. That is one more reason for a dog to not trust them. I try to sleep, but the feeling that my ship and I are in danger fills the air like the stink of bilge water.

CHAPTER 4

Bahía Santa Lucía, Brazil

November–December 1519

At last a brisk wind sweeps the ships westward across the sea. The North Star vanishes when we cross the equator. Sailors speak of this line that circles the world, cutting it in half. It is nothing that a dog can see.

Now the armada is in the southern half of the world. Many of the crew have never been this far. They wait for the southern sea to turn red and boil or keep fearful watch for eighty-foot eels—legends that have been passed from sailor to sailor.

The real monsters are the *bichos* on the ship. Lice burrow into scalps and fleas bite flesh. Worms bore into the wooden hull. Weevils infest the biscuits. Cockroaches chew on the rigging. I try to keep the mice and rats at bay, but new litters are born faster than I can catch them.

I am patiently stalking a cunning rat that makes its home under the capstan when Marco, Enrique, and Pigafetta saunter across the deck. "Magellan has set a course to the New World," Pigafetta tells the other two.

"Why is it new?" Marco carries Pigafetta's journal and writing instruments as well as a rolled-up parchment. The boy now appears to serve the scribe.

The rat pops his head out, sees us, and disappears. Sighing, I flop in the sun.

"I have not seen the wondrous map created in 1502 by the German Waldseemuller, but he calls the strip of land across the Ocean Sea 'America,'" Pigafetta says. "He named it after the explorer Amerigo Vespucci. The crew is grumbling that we will never reach the Spice Islands, but Magellan is certain we can. He believes there is a passage that will lead us to a western ocean and thus the Spice Islands." He rolls up the map and smiles. "Perhaps when we find it, we will claim even greater treasures for Spain."

"Gold and silver?" Marco's eyes are huge.

"For me, treasure would be finding the land where I was born," Enrique says.

"Do you remember what it was named?" Pigafetta asks.

Enrique shakes his head. "I was sold to my master from a slave market in China when I was young. I only remember palm trees and warm sand and being carried off against my will."

"Are you going to be a slave forever?" Marco asks.

"The captain general is giving me my freedom when he dies," Enrique says. "He tells me it is in his will."

Pigafetta tucks the map under his arm. "Perhaps we can find your home."

A raindrop plops on my nose, and I look up.

Once again clouds are forming. The last storms are in the distant past, and this rain will be a godsend.

As the drops hit the deck, the men drag out wooden buckets to fill for drinking and washing. We are surrounded by seawater, but the salt makes skin itch and clothes stiff. When a bucket is partly filled, I jump in to splash off the stink of the ship. Dias chases me off.

"*Tierra!* Land ahead!" a sailor hollers from the crow's nest high above us.

Sailors drop their soap and rags and hurry to the bow. The ship is swiftly approaching an inlet surrounded by green hills.

"Is this the New World?" Enrique asks excitedly.

"If the map is correct, this is Verzin," Pigafetta says. Though rain drips from the brim of his hat onto his nose, his eyes are alight at the sight of land. "Magellan calls it *Brazil*, the name the Portuguese gave it because of the country's brazilwood trees. The Portuguese have a factory here. But I see none of Portugal's ships in harbor."

As the *Trinidad* nears the land, dark-skinned women row canoes out to meet us. The crew cheers.

"Will the natives be friendly?" Marco eyes the women. Some sailors are climbing down rope ladders to reach them. Others haul in the longboat that we tow to bring it closer to the ship.

Pigafetta shakes his head. "They appear friendly. But I believe Amerigo Vespucci wrote about cannibalism when he visited in 1502."

Marco's jaw drops. I do not know the word *cannibalism*, but it must be something fearsome.

Pigafetta laughs again. "Do not fear being eaten, *niño*. Carvalho, the pilot from the *Concepción*, lived here many years ago. He has taught me some words. The people call themselves *Aba. Taisse* is the Aba word for knife and *pinda* means fishhook."

"Prepare to land!" Espinosa shouts. Magellan hurries from his cabin to the quarterdeck. He calls out more commands, but the men are beyond orders as they scramble over the sides to climb down to the women in the canoes bobbing below.

"We will name this bay Bahía Santa Lucía in honor of the saint who is celebrated today," Magellan calls out before turning toward the ladder that has been dropped down to the longboat.

"If Magellan is going to disembark, I am going with him." Pigafetta sets off toward the stern. "I want to communicate with the Aba."

Marco hurries after him and I follow. After months at sea, a chance to be on shore is not to be missed.

I stare down at the water, knowing I cannot make the long drop. On other voyages we have sometimes anchored in a bay shallow enough for me to be able to swim. But the *Trinidad* is too far from shore.

Suddenly Beast wraps one of his arms around me, and I feel myself headed downward. Marco scrambles after us and into the longboat.

Espinosa scoffs. "Perhaps the natives will trade pineapples for a rat-catching dog," he says. "I hear it is delicious—dog meat, not the fruit."

I hide behind Beast's giant legs until the longboat reaches shore. As soon as the bottom of the boat scrapes sand, I jump into the surf. A few paddles and I am on the shore.

The group from the *Trinidad* climbs out and greets the natives. Other sailors have arrived in the canoes paddled by the women. The men of Brazil are olive-skinned, with bones sticking out from their noses and lips. Two wear headpieces made of feathers. All carry bows and arrows. I am not interested in being cooked, so I steer clear of the humans and race toward the line of trees.

The forest is shady and alive with buzzes and chirps. My first quest is to find fresh water. Always we are parched on the ship. I follow an animal trail that winds to a small stream. I lap eagerly then roll in a small pool, my legs kicking the air.

Hungry, I snap up crunchy grasshoppers as they leap into the air. Then I dig up fat, wiggly larvae from under a rotted stump.

I stay within hearing range of the beach. My ears are keen, and humans are noisy. Even though the cool of the forest is tempting, the ship is my home and I don't want to get left behind.

As I head back in the direction of the beach, I find a juicy fruit that has fallen from above. It has split open and the yellow flesh inside is delicious.

A scrambling whoosh through the leaves makes me look up. Tiny faces stare down at me. They seem almost human, with beady eyes and flat noses. Each brown face is surrounded by an orange mane of hair.

My own hair bristles. The animals have long arms and legs that cling to the branches and trunks. They cluck angrily as if telling me to go away. One of the creatures would be no problem for even a sea-weary dog to fight. But there are many hanging above me as if ready to pounce.

Slowly I back away, baring my teeth to show how fierce I am. I have seen monkeys before on other voyages. They are crafty and quick and sometimes mean. These creatures look and act like monkeys, and I can

tell from their faces that I may have to run or fight.

Sharp clapping behind me sends them scampering high into the trees. "Go away!" someone hollers, and I recognize Marco's voice. "Leave Leo the Brave alone!" He shakes a stick in the air, and the creatures disappear in the canopy of leaves.

"Why did you run off when we landed?" Marco asks me.

Turning tail, I finish eating my fruit. I did not ask the skinny boy to watch over me. I was not afraid to fight the furry creatures.

He grabs up one of the fruits and begins to eat too. Juice runs down his chin. "Delicious. These must be the mangoes that Pigafetta spoke of. Magellan is trading tiny bells for baskets of them. The Aba have chicken and geese too," he goes on. "The crew will feast while we are anchored here."

Squatting next to me, Marco sighs. "Brazil might not be the Spice Islands, but it is close to paradise. *Signore* Pigafetta says we are far from the Moluccas, but I hope it is not much longer. Life on board is not grand. In truth, you and the *signore* are the only friends I have."

Raising my head, I hear the rise and fall of human voices growing closer. It is time to go. I hurry from the forest.

I know Marco is behind me, but I do not glance to make sure he gets to the boat safely. Sailing the Ocean Sea brings many dangers. I have saved Marco twice. Now he thinks he has rescued me from a band of monkeys. Perhaps that is what he means by *friends.*

I hop into the longboat, which is piled with baskets of fruit. Chickens, their feet trussed, flap and cackle in the stern.

"A stay in Brazil will do the crew good," Pigafetta tells Magellan.

"True. The men need fresh food and a rest," Magellan agrees. "But we cannot anchor here long. We will be sailing south along the coast even though it soon will be winter. I am determined to find the passage to the Spice Islands."

Pigafetta nods. "I am certain that you, Captain General, will be the first to find one."

"The first in the name of King Charles and our Almighty Lord," Magellan says. "We will claim the strait and any new lands thereafter. Then we will find our way west to the Moluccas—and around the world."

Around the world. From the awe shining in Pigafetta's eyes, I sense that the *Trinidad*, its crew, and I, the lowly rat dog, may achieve something wonderful.

CHAPTER 5

Brazil to Port Saint Julian

January–August 1520

Though they are refreshed, the crew is sullen when we depart Brazil. We are leaving warm breezes and friendly natives for a mysterious passage called a *strait*.

As we head south, winter descends, and our harshest days are soon upon us.

The sailors don tar-coated capes and pull their caps tighter around their heads. But buffeted by hail, snow, and surf, we are always cold and wet. My hair grows thicker to protect me from the icy storms.

Marco has created a new nest higher up in the hull,

farther from the bilge water that sloshes and stinks. He has lined the space with a fur that he traded the Aba for a knife and he covers himself with a blanket that was a present from Pigafetta. I drag in a ripped canvas sail and join him there. We are just bunkmates, I tell myself. We keep each other warm, which means surviving another day.

At night Marco reads aloud from *The Travels of Marco Polo*. I do not understand his words, but the hum of his voice is comforting, not hard like the sailors'.

Tonight, though, I hear worry in his voice. "I cannot go back to Spain, Leo," he tells me. "Captain General Magellan wants to circle the world and return to Spain, but I stole this book from the nuns before I ran off. I am a *ladron*, a thief, and if I set foot on Spanish soil again, I will go to prison forever."

He pushes up a sleeve and shows me his red scars. "Though prison I can likely endure. It cannot be worse than the nuns' whippings," he adds with a heavy sigh.

I sigh too, for in truth, as a ship's dog, I know these frigid waters may be worse than either prison or the nuns' whippings. On other voyages the icy seas and long hours of work claimed many lives. Only the hardiest survived. Shivering, I curl closer to Marco, hoping that the weather's punishing cruelty won't last.

≈

But the days grow shorter and the nights grow colder as the armada explores every inlet and bay. The men on board grow despondent—except for Magellan.

"We will find the passage!" our leader assures the weary crew. "And soon we will bask in the warmth of the Spice Islands."

"Is he right?" Marco asks Pigafetta when no one else can hear. "The sailors whisper that Magellan is leading us to our deaths."

Pigafetta frowns. "Magellan has a vision—and a plan. Ignore the whispers."

"But I have heard the word *mutiny* again," Marco continues.

"The treasoners Cartagena and de la Reina have been locked in *Victoria*'s barred cabin for months," Pigafetta says. "If others are speaking of mutiny, I have not heard. We must trust our leader and not the grumblings of a disgruntled crew."

At night I sneak around the ship, listening for these angry words. Hernando wraps frostbitten fingers and sets broken arms. Steward checks hatch locks and counts food barrels. Sailors roll bone dice and wash filthy tunics. I do not catch anyone on the *Trinidad* defying Magellan, and I breathe easier that my ship is safe from human foibles—at least for now.

One day we sail between two small islands that appear seemingly alone in the vast waters. Strange creatures sun themselves on the rocky beach and swim nearby. I set my front paws on the railings and bark at them. They are black and white and swift swimmers.

"I believe those are a type of goose," Pigafetta tells Marco.

My hair bristles since I have never seen a goose that stands upright like a man.

"And those are sea wolves," Pigafetta adds, pointing to strange silvery gray, slick animals basking on the same rocks.

One raises its head and "barks," and I notice its teeth are not sharp and it has no claws.

"Whatever they are, they look good to eat," Marco says as he licks his lips.

Already Espinosa is ordering a hunting party to go ashore. Later that night we feast on geese and sea wolves.

Our stomachs full, we continue south along the coast. But storms continue to batter the ships.

During one pounding rain, Marco and the other pages sponge water from a pool with rags and wring them out over the railing. My ears are flattened by the pelting drops as I inspect the dead remains of the cookfire. Above me in the masts, sailors fight the ropes and sails that whip in the wind. Others are below, manning the bilge pumps. All are sodden, half-frozen, and muttering angrily about the miserable weather.

Magellan strides from his cabin dressed in an oiled cape. He peers from bow to stern and then shouts to Espinosa so all can hear. "We must find shelter before the fierce winds and waves break our hulls into pieces. Order the pilots into the bay ahead!"

The crew gives a half-hearted cheer. The *Trinidad* signals the other ships and the armada limps into a harbor cradled by gray cliffs. There the ships drop anchor.

Marco and I peer over the railing. Through the mist we spot geese and sea wolves on the shores. Below us, fish flash in the rain-splattered water. I drool, knowing we will not go hungry if we wait here for the weather to calm.

Magellan calls this Port Saint Julian after the saint. "We will winter here," he tells the crew, who have been ordered on deck. This brings some grateful murmurs but then our leader adds, "It may be a long and grueling stay, so food and drink will be rationed."

The murmurs turn into a fierce roar that rises from the sailors, and I cower alongside the railing, trying to stay away from their raised fists.

"For seven weeks we have braved the weather!" one sailor yells. "And this is how you reward us?"

Dias steps forward. "Captain General, we demand that you lead us back to Spain before we die of hunger or in a storm."

The others nod in agreement.

Magellan throws back his shoulders, and by his side, Espinosa rattles his sword. I glimpse Pigafetta, who is standing behind the two men.

"We will not go back," Magellan declares. "My quest to find a passage will not be stopped. Before we left, I made a promise to King Charles."

Diego climbs onto the capstan. "Surely King Charles would not wish for us to perish!" he says.

Sharp words ring from bow to stern.

"If there even is a passage!"

"Do not our lives have value?"

"We have been searching and searching in vain!"

I can feel the anger in the air, which is more chilling than the cold. Marco crouches and laces his fingers in my fur. "Is this mutiny?" he whispers in my ear.

The sailors are surging toward Magellan when suddenly Pigafetta steps forward and whispers in Magellan's ear. Our leader nods and again addresses the crew.

"The *Trinidad, Victoria, San Antonio,* and *Concepción* will remain in the harbor patching up the ships and gathering supplies," he says. "I will send the speedier *Santiago* to search for the passage."

The sailors frown but slowly they disband, as if our leader's plan has appeased them. Marco lets out a relieved breath, as do I.

Days later, the entire crew of the *Trinidad* hugs the railing to watch as the *Santiago* leaves the bay, sails flapping. It is the first time there have not been five ships in the armada. I watch it disappear, the mast finally dipping below the horizon.

While we wait for its return, our crew—under Espinosa's harsh command—gets the ship in order.

Decks are caulked. Brass fittings polished. The bow scraped. Sails mended. All this is accomplished with frostbitten fingers. Even I become stiff from the cold, and the rats often outrun me.

Marco grows thinner. Pigafetta cannot protect him from the brutality of life at sea, and as always, provisions are low. The boy scrubs ice-covered decks by day. At night he takes his turn at watch, flipping the sand clocks every half hour. Often I keep watch with him, a straw pallet our only protection from the cold. *"Al cuarto!"* he cries out when his shift is over. "On deck!" At that, the sleepy-eyed dawn watch staggers from below to take his place.

Only then do Marco and I retreat to our raggedy nest for a few hours' rest. There we huddle against each other, sharing our warmth. Sometimes Marco tries to read; often his teeth are chattering too wildly, and we are so exhausted we fall into a leaden sleep.

I have survived four other voyages, but I was younger then, and the trips weren't so harsh and so long. Will Marco make it to the New World? Will I?

The boy has youth on his side, but perhaps this will be my last journey.

CHAPTER 6

Port Saint Julian

June–July 1520

Weeks go by and the *Santiago* does not return. Magellan paces the deck. Pigafetta paces with him while Enrique, Marco, and I stride behind. The silence is tense, and worry fills the air.

"Might they be lost?" Pigafetta finally asks.

"More like they sailed back to Spain as mutinous cowards!" Magellan exclaims, but then stops himself as if he has said too much.

"Or perhaps storms have blown the ship off course," Pigafetta suggests. Magellan grunts and scans the bay once again.

My attention is not on a lost ship but on movement on land. Faint noises come from the shore, and they are not the barks of sea wolves nor the gaks of geese. Then something red waves in the air.

I set up a fierce baying. "Hush, *cao!*" Magellan hollers, but Marco sees it too.

"Someone is on the beach," the boy insists.

Magellan swings around. "I did not authorize a party to go ashore."

"It is two men," Pigafetta says, "and by the looks of the *bonete* one is waving, they are sailors."

Magellan orders a crew to row the longboat to pick up the men. Dias, Diego, and Beast volunteer. Marco and I hug the railing, watching the longboat as it glides toward shore.

"For certain, they are sailors," Marco says to me. "But are they from the *Santiago?* If so, why are they on land? And where are the others?"

No one knows the answer, and it seems ages before the longboat comes back with the two men. Magellan waits by the door of his cabin as they are helped up the rope ladder. "Bring them to me," he orders.

Pigafetta accompanies one while Espinosa guides the second. The rescued men's beards are long and ice-crusted. Their wrapped fingers are bloody, and their bodies are gaunt beneath their ragged capes.

"It is Faleiro and Juan from the *Santiago!*" Espinosa calls out as the four make their way across the deck.

The two survivors do not speak, but give a shaky bow when they meet Magellan. He ushers them into his cabin. Pigafetta has been summoned to write their tale and Hernando to apply oil to their fingers and cheeks. Espinosa stands guard by the door, but I slip inside on the heels of the scribe.

Enrique has set out a fine meal of goose and cheese with a special treat of almonds and quince jelly. My mouth waters at the wonderful smells.

"Eat while telling us what happened to the *Santiago*," Magellan says, settling into a chair at the head of his table.

"As we were exploring, a storm came upon us so suddenly that we had no time to reef the sails," Faleiro says between cracked lips.

"The wind caught the sails and pushed us into the rocks, which tore open the hull," Juan adds as he stuffs handfuls of food into his mouth. "The *Santiago* took on water and we thought it would sink." He crosses himself with a grease-smeared finger. "Luck was with us—the wind pushed the ship to shore before it broke up."

"One by one we crawled to the end of the jib boom and jumped to the beach," Faleiro says. "Thirty-seven of us. None were lost."

Magellan nods but does not interrupt.

"The *Santiago* was swept to sea," Juan adds. "Nothing was left but a few planks."

"We couldn't stay without provisions," Faleiro continues. "We hiked over snowy mountains until we reached a wide river. We made a raft from the planks. But only two could fit on the raft, so Captain Serrano appointed us to cross and find help by land."

Faleiro pats me, and then, shivering, he raises his mug and gulps his wine.

Tears fill Juan's eyes. "Now thirty-five of our

crew wait for us to save them. It is a four- or five-day journey through perilous wilderness."

Abruptly Magellan stands. "Eat and rest, my heroes. You will lead a rescue party and we will find them."

A chunk of goose falls by Faleiro's feet and I quickly snap it up.

Suddenly Espinosa sees me. His eyes grow dark, as if I am some enemy. "Dirty dog!" Seizing me by the scruff of the neck, he holds me up. "You dare to steal our guests' food?"

I snarl and squirm, but I cannot get away.

Pigafetta stops writing. "Excuse Leo's intrusion," he tells Espinosa in his calm voice. "He is a curious dog."

"Leo! The ratter has a name?" Espinosa scoffs. I bare my teeth at him and he laughs. "Perhaps his name should be Shark Food. I will toss him into the sea once and for all."

The water of Port Saint Julian is so cold that at least I will die instantly.

With a nasty grin Espinosa opens the cabin door.
Pigafetta rises, but I know the scribe does not have
the authority to save me.

"Let the dog go," Magellan says. "As long as he
does his job of killing rats, he serves his purpose.
Besides, we have more pressing issues—to rescue the
other men from the *Santiago*."

Espinosa blows out an angry breath but obeys.
He sends me out the door with a swift boot. Marco

is outside, as if waiting for word on the fate of the *Santiago*. He grabs me by the scruff. "Did you incur the wrath of Espinosa?" he asks.

I pull away from him. The ship creaks and groans like a living beast as I escape to my nest deep in its belly. I have worked hard to do my job to keep it free from *bichos,* but Espinosa has reminded me that I have gotten too close to the people who man the ship.

Curling up, I tuck my nose under my tail. If I am to survive the rest of this perilous voyage, I must keep my own company again. That means focusing on *bichos* and not worrying about humans.

❧

The next day Magellan picks twenty-four strong men to rescue the crew from the *Santiago*. Many days pass and finally the frigid air begins to warm and the days grow longer. A leak in the *Trinidad*'s hull is repaired. Sails are patched and stitched.

But as the men work, a gloom settles over the ship and the question hangs in the cold air like fog: will the sailors from the *Santiago* return alive? Even Magellan worriedly scans the horizon for signs of the rescue party that went ashore.

I am searching for a crafty rat who has survived the winter when calls from the shore prick my ears. Quickly I trot to the railing. Marco has been hanging on a shroud, fixing a tear with new rope. He shouts, "The rescuers have returned!"

The crew drops their work and hurries to the railing. On the shore, the sailors from the *Santiago* and the team of rescuers wave their *bonetes*.

Cheers resound as the *Trinidad* crew waves back. Sailors link arms and dance around the deck. Marco hugs me and then we twirl and whirl in happiness at the sight of the returning men.

It is the first joy the ship has seen in a long time.

CHAPTER 7

Leaving Port Saint Julian

August 1520

Hearing the uproar, Magellan hurries from his cabin. His face lights when he spots the men on shore. "Send the longboats to retrieve them!" he commands. Then he orders the crew to stop frolicking. "Bring food, wine, and blankets to the main deck so we may be prepared to greet our survivors."

Soon the men arrive. The sailors from the *Santiago* are pale-faced and thin, but quickly rally now that they are safe. Amazingly, none of the survivors were lost during the journey.

We hover around them as they gulp down goose and *bizcocho* and tell tales of the shipwreck.

"We dug shellfish in the river."

"Ate ferns and roots."

"When the rescuers arrived, we thought they were angels."

"Who knew that hardtack could taste so delicious," one sailor says, which brings laughter from the listeners.

"When we left the river with the rescuers, there was only ice to quench our thirst."

"And deep snow to pluck at our feet and souls."

After they have dined, Magellan divides the crew of the *Santiago* among the four ships. Serrano is appointed captain of the *Concepción*.

Magellan then orders the armada readied for departure from the bay. This should be a relief, but I once again sense a wary tenseness. Sailors grumble to each other about long hours and sparse food. Petty fights break out. The joy the crew felt at the return of the survivors was brief, and their simmering anger again bubbles to the surface.

Pigafetta and Marco sense these troubles too.

"Magellan is making sure that all the captains will be loyal to him," Pigafetta explains while he eats his sparse meal of salted goose and stale biscuit. Marco crouches by the scribe's lone chair and I sit on the other side, always eager when food is around.

"His first cousin Alvaro de Mesquita has taken over command of the *San Antonio*, and *Victoria* will be captained by his brother-in-law Duarte Barbosa," Pigafetta continues. "This has made the demoted Spanish captains angry."

"The sailors are angry as well," Marco says. "They rightly complain that Magellan may be leading us to our deaths in his quest for this passage."

"Yes, the captain general is fiercely determined to find a way to the Spice Islands," Pigafetta agrees. "I hold his skill and daring in the highest regard. Others do not. We have been anchored in the bay for months and now we are setting off into the unknown. It does appear that Magellan is sending us to an icy grave." He sighs and hands Marco his half-full wooden bowl. Marco shares the contents with me.

Even a mistrustful dog gives in when dried goose is involved.

Pigafetta dabs his mouth with a grimy handkerchief. "Magellan has also confided that he will carry out his punishment on the mutinous Cartagena and the priest Sanchez de la Reina," he continues. "He wants all those who are disloyal to see that they will be severely dealt with."

Marco scrapes the last of the food with his fingers as he says, "I fear that will only fuel the crew's resentment."

I eagerly lick the bowl. Even though I hear the concern in Marco's voice, a meal that isn't a rat makes me happy.

Before the armada leaves, Magellan orders Cartagena and de la Reina to be brought to the *Trinidad*. When the two arrive in the longboat, hands shackled, Espinosa parades them across the deck for all the crew to see. Marco and I watch as he forces the two men to their knees.

Magellan climbs onto the forecastle, standing above us all. He is dressed in his finery, and the wind ruffles the plume in his hat as he announces, "Juan de Cartegena and Pero Sanchez de la Reina, you are convicted of mutiny. Under the laws of Spain and King Charles, I, captain general of the fleet, will levy punishment. You will forthwith be removed from the *Trinidad* and left to fend for yourselves on the shores of Port Saint Julian."

A gasp rises from the crew at the severity of the sentence. Cartagena raises his head. "But sir…"

His protest is halted as Espinosa jerks him to his feet and hustles the two condemned men into the longboat.

On the quarterdeck, the pilots holler instructions to the rest of the crew. "Raise the anchors! Climb the foremast! Prepare the sails!"

The cannons boom messages to the other ships. Marco scurries up a shroud to help unfurl a sail. Pigafetta and I step out of the way of the busy sailors. Perhaps that is why we are the only ones to watch as the longboat drops Cartegena and de la Reina on the beach with a small cache of hardtack and wine. Perhaps we are the only ones to hear their pleading cries as the longboat rows back to the *Trinidad*.

But I do not think so. The rest of the officers and crew cast frightened glances toward the shore.

Magellan has gotten revenge on two of the men who declared mutiny. And he has sent a powerful warning to anyone who might defy him.

CHAPTER 8

Finding the Strait

August–November 1520

The passage of time is hazy for a sea dog. From the countless days and nights, the dwindling supplies, and the growth of the sailors' beards, I can tell that we have been at sea longer than any other voyage I have been on.

The armada seems stuck in an endless search along a frigid, barren coast. The sailors signed on for the warmth and bounty of the Spice Islands, and their complaints are as thick as the frost in their hair.

The four remaining ships continue down the coast. "The strait," I keep hearing Pigafetta and

Magellan say. We search every inlet and channel and are sorely disappointed when each ends in shallow or briny water.

Finally I hear a cry of excitement from the forecastle. Sailors gather along the rail, bundled in their raggedy capes, which have been mended and remended. All of us stare in wonder at a glassy, wide-mouthed bay that seems to have no end. Could this be the mysterious strait?

"Note this in your log," Magellan says to the pilot. "At 52 degrees latitude, we have sighted a vast, watery opening that appears to wind its way deep through the land."

"Look on the bank!" Marco points at giant bones poking into the sky.

"Whale skeletons," Pigafetta announces as he sketches in his journal. "This may be proof that this inlet is a migration route to the ocean on the other side."

As the ships sail into the waterway, Magellan

shouts to the sounders, "Keep checking the depth of the water!"

"No bottom is found!" one calls back.

The pilot hollers for a westward course. "Keep the *Trinidad* steady in the swirling tides!"

I can't take my eyes off the curve of bones that rises above the shore. "These whales must be monsters," Marco whispers.

"God's creatures, not mythological ones," Pigafetta observes. He pokes Marco's bony side. "You have ribs just like the whales. And if we have finally found the strait, one more myth will be reality. The cartographers will soon map the true existence of a passage west."

As we sail deeper into the opening, I keep my eyes on the land surrounding us. Gray clouds hang over the water and shroud the mountaintops. The air is frosty, the shores barren. Wildlife does not welcome our ships. There are no signs of life at all.

Our leader has endlessly searched for this strait. Yet even a dog can worry that this dark passage may not lead the ship and its crew to the riches of the Spice Islands, but instead to our deaths.

After days of traveling through the strait, which seems to stretch forever, triumph turns to caution. Magellan has ordered the longboats to pick up the captains and pilots from the other ships, and they gather on the quarterdeck for a meeting. Pigafetta joins them, his journal in hand and Marco by his side.

"I fear that what I once thought was correct is wrong," Magellan tells the officers. "There is no one smooth waterway west, but a maze of inlets and rivers. We have provisions for three more months. My hopes are that the supplies are enough to carry us through to the other side, and thus to the Spice Islands."

"That hope is folly," one of the pilots says sternly. "We must return to Spain for provisions first. The crew is spent. The ships are worn. Even if we find a western ocean, no explorer has crossed it before.

It may take longer to reach the Moluccas than you believe."

Magellan shakes his head. "We have come this far and will move forward at all costs. I will send the *San Antonio* and *Concepción* ahead to find the best way."

Captains Serrano of the *Concepción* and de Mesquita of the *San Antonio* exchange angry glances, and I feel the tension radiating from the others. Even Pigafetta stops writing.

The pilots storm off, followed by de Mesquita and Serrano.

The next day the two ships sail west under Magellan's orders to find "the best way." While we wait for them to return, I watch sea elephants lolling on a rocky beach. They are long and fat and have no legs or fur. With flat arms they pull their bulk into the water, where they glide gracefully among the icy waves.

The sailors use nets to catch fish, which shine like dagger blades when they are dragged on deck. I snatch up one or two each time, eager for a fresh meal. Soon they will be dried, salted, and stored under Steward's watchful eye.

One morning a huge shadow sails over our ship, darkening the deck. With cries of fear the sailors flatten themselves against the wood and hide under tarps. A giant bird, wings spread, flies above the mainmast. I bark ferociously, telling it to keep its distance, and it veers away. Pigafetta draws a picture of it in his journal. In the distance we can see others soaring around the mountain ranges. None of us have ever seen birds so huge, and we hope they portend good luck.

Finally guns announce the return of the *Concepción*. The ship's longboat brings the captain and pilot to the *Trinidad*.

Captain Serrano bows to Magellan when they meet. "We have explored and found many inlets leading nowhere; the pilot has created a map showing where not to sail." He waves at the other man, who unfurls a parchment. "This will at least keep us on the best course."

"And where is the *San Antonio*?" Magellan asks.

The captain shakes his head. "We lost sight of her several days in."

Magellan stalks off, Pigafetta by his side. "This is not acceptable," he mutters. "My cousin is captain of the ship. Did he dare defy my orders and sail back to Spain? Or did his crew mutiny and force him to change direction?"

Pigafetta tries to reassure him. "Let us wait and see, Captain General. Perhaps the *San Antonio* is simply lost in the maze that Serrano has described."

We wait, but the ship, its crew, and its supplies have disappeared.

Finally Magellan orders a banner planted on a windswept dune. A letter stating our course is buried beneath it, in case the *San Antonio* returns. The large carrack carried sturdy sailors and ample supplies, which will be missed.

The next day, only three ships set sail. "Westward!" Magellan announces the course. It seems he is the only person certain that the passage will lead to the Spice Islands.

Countless days and nights after the ships entered the strait, I hear cries of excitement. Marco and I scamper from our nest and up through the hatch to see what's going on.

The entire crew is on deck. It is dawn and some of the sailors are wiping sleep from their eyes. Others are holding cards, dice, or hardtack. All are staring ahead in silence.

I trot to the forecastle and peer past the bowsprit. Fog masks the sky ahead, but I hear the thunderous crash of waves on rock. The air is salty and gulls swoop and dive.

Slowly the fog lifts. Two spits of land rise on either side of us, craggy with cliffs. Beyond them, the sea stretches to the horizon.

"We have done it!" Magellan exclaims. "It has taken thirty-eight days to navigate the strait, but we found a passage." Tears are streaming down his cheeks. "This spit will be named Cape Desire, for we have been desiring it for so long."

"Wednesday, November 28, 1520," Pigafetta murmurs as he writes in his journal, "we sailed into the western sea."

Beside me Marco shivers. I do not blame him. We have made our way through the mysterious strait and reached the end. Ahead of us is truly the unknown. The western sea is dark, wind-whipped, frothy— and *endless*. I tremble, my senses telling me that our journey and its perils have just begun.

CHAPTER 9

Across the Western Sea

November 1520–March 1521

The three ships seem to fly across the western ocean.

"The captain general believes we will reach the Spice Islands any day," Pigafetta assures Marco.

When we were sailing off the western coast, we were able to catch flying fish and albacore. But now the water is too deep and dark for fish. Since turning seaward, there has been no sight of land.

Maggots ate the last of the salted cod and seals. Next they wiggled to the sails, munching their way through hemp and cotton. Even the hungry sailors have taken to chewing the leather wrappings on the yards.

Pigafetta hands Marco a chunk of wormy biscuit slathered with quince jelly from his dwindling stash. The boy tears it in half and hands me part. My portion is gone in one bite, and Marco's belly growls. His ribs show beneath his threadbare tunic. Pigafetta's overgown flaps loosely.

These two have been sharing their food with me. It is time I pay them back.

Rats can grow fat on waste and wood. Patiently I wait, catching two plump ones. Tails sticking from my mouth, I carry them to the top deck and drop them at Pigafetta's feet. He stares at them in surprise. Marco snatches them up, peels off their hides with a knife, and laces them on a spit. Soon their flesh is roasting over the cookfire.

The smell brings the other sailors. "Get the dog to catch me a rat," Diego says as he pulls a *ducado* from his pocket. "I will pay." His gums are swollen and sores dot his hands.

"I as well." Dias flashes a pack of cards. "This is all I have to trade." His fingers holding the cards are thick, his body is stooped, and he has few teeth left.

Soon I am bringing dead rats for everyone, until Espinosa saunters over to see what the commotion is.

"Oh ho!" He grabs me by the scruff before I can dodge him. "The rats may be plump, but this dog is plumper. Think how tasty he will be roasted over the coals," he says as he holds me up in the air. "I think I will string him up from the yardarm."

"No!" Marco protests. He throws a weak punch, but Espinosa backhands him and the boy falls to the deck.

Diego gives Espinosa a murderous look and picks up Marco.

"How dare you strike an officer, you miserable stowaway!" Espinosa thunders. "And you, Diego, do not defend him. You will both be cooked with the dog. Three fewer mouths to feed and a feast for us."

Pigafetta stands. "Good master, forgive their rashness. The dog and the boy are providing a much-needed service to the crew. Diego and the others are starving. Can you not have pity on them?"

"Pity?" Espinosa scoffs. "It is the unhealthy air that affects these men. Hard work in the sun will cure them." He releases his hold on me and I drop with a loud thud on the deck. Espinosa strikes Diego, who grimaces in pain. Then he shoves Dias, who is so weak he almost stumbles, into the coals of the cookfire. "So disband. Magellan will tolerate no slackers."

I slink behind a crate. My hatred for Espinosa is growing. His cruelty is aimed at everyone, and I snarl as I watch him stride off, shouting to the men.

At the same time a new feeling is growing inside of me—a sense of kinship with Marco, Pigafetta, and other crew members. But I know I must shake off this new feeling; it is too dangerous to trust people. So I busy myself catching another rat, snapping its neck with one bite. I bring it to Marco.

"This is another one for Diego," he says, "for standing up to Espinosa." He spits on the deck when he says the name.

Pigafetta frowns as if thinking hard. "Espinosa is wrong about unhealthy air. It is disease that ails these men. A disease that weakens the teeth, limbs, and body until death overtakes them. Vasco de Gama wrote of the malady when it befell his crew in 1498." He sighs deeply. "Worse, our leader has no command over illness, and I fear that soon our ship will be burying many of its men."

That night Dias dies.

The crew is grave. The men have withstood so many hardships, but this new one—this wasting disease—has them cowed. They gather round as Diego and Beast wrap Dias's body in a tattered tarp and tie two cannonballs to his feet.

Magellan praises Dias in a prayer. Then Diego and Beast lift the body onto a plank, which they tilt over the edge of the ship's railing until Dias slides off it and plunges into the water with a splash.

Pigafetta crosses himself. Marco utters a Hail Mary.

As we continue westward, twenty-eight more sailors die. There are so many bodies that soon there is a brief prayer, no tarp, and simply a splash. No one stops working. No one has an explanation. Even Espinosa grows silent as the disease works its way through the *Trinidad*.

The Lord graces Pigafetta, Magellan, Enrique, Marco, and me with good health. Most of the other captains and officers stay well too. It is the blessings of St. Elmo, they say, but the sailors and other pages, who are pocked with boils and plagued with bleeding gums, do not want to hear that they are not so blessed.

Magellan gives some bottles of medicine to Hernando, who treats the men as best as he can. But the medicine has no effect, and the disease marches through the three ships until only a ghostly crew mans the sails and rigging.

Finally an island is spotted in the distance. Those who can still move stagger to the railing. The small mound is bare of trees and birds. The only creatures in sight are huge sharks, which circle the ship. I back away, fearful that Espinosa will fling me into the sea.

Though exhausted and sick, Diego and Beast catch two of the sharks. Even though the meat is tough and stringy, the men feast that night. Marco slips me a tasty chunk.

Still, we must leave this barren island to find safe

harbor. More days of sun and illness go by. Soon water and wine are running low.

Even Magellan, who has not given up on his quest for the Spice Islands, grows despondent. He flings his maps overboard. "With the pardon of the cartographers, the Moluccas are not to be found!"

"The mapmakers never ventured this far," Pigafetta reassures him. "You are the first to find the western sea. We have made fifty or sixty leagues each day. It has been ninety-eight days since we left the strait. Soon the Indes will be reached. You will see."

"They must be reached or we will perish," Magellan whispers.

"*Tierra!*" suddenly rings from the lookout. "*Tierra! Tierra!*"

Magellan climbs up the mast to see for himself. I jump onto a crate to look over the railing.

Two islands are in the distance. As we glide into the clear water of a bay, Pigafetta sketches the scene before us.

"The islands look large enough to have rabbit or pineapples!" Marco exclaims. "We will eat at last. Can they be the Spice Islands, *Signore?*"

Pigafetta shakes his head. "I do not know, but what I do know is that they are our deliverance. Without fresh food and water, we are doomed."

"This island is similar to where I was born," Enrique says excitedly. "Perhaps we have reached the Moluccas."

Lifting my nose, I sniff the air. It is filled with the scents of plants and flowers. I dream of mangoes and freshwater streams, but then my keen eyes spot specks of movement.

The lookout in the crow's nest has spotted them too. "*Indios!*"

Small canoes with triangle sails skim toward us across the ocean waves. They zigzag through the water, quickly surrounding the three ships. Standing in the skiffs are tall olive-skinned men. They wear palm-leaf hats and have long black hair to their waists. They do not shout friendly greetings as in Brazil. Instead they carry spears that they thrust at the *Trinidad*'s hull.

I bark, warning the crew of danger. But weak and unsteady from disease and hunger, the sailors can only stare in horror.

CHAPTER 10

Isle of Thieves

March 1521

The natives nimbly climb ropes to reach the deck of the *Trinidad*. I swirl about their bare feet, snapping at their heels. They ignore me and the protesting sailors. Even Espinosa and Magellan are overcome as the natives swarm like ants from bow to stern.

One snatches the iron pot from the cookfire. Holding it in the air, he crows with delight. Others grab ropes, pulleys, chains, knives, and spoons. One brazenly snatches the pen from Pigafetta's grasp. Marco tries to get it back, but the native only brushes him off as if he is a pesky fly.

Then one lifts the hatch and shouts to the others. Chattering excitedly, they disappear below.

"Arm yourselves!" Magellan finally rouses himself to shout an order.

"No, no weapons," Pigafetta implores him. "The natives are no threat. They only want our things."

"The thieves cannot have them!" Espinosa grabs a machete and starts across the deck to the hatch. An *indio* climbs out, his arms laden with several cannonballs. Espinosa slaps the man's cheek.

Startled, the man drops the cannonballs and slaps the master-at-arms right back. Espinosa growls, and when the *indio* turns to pick up his loot, Espinosa cuts him in the back with the machete.

Crying out, the *indio* flings himself overboard. Streaming from the hatch, the others follow, diving into the sea and swimming to their boats.

After climbing into their canoes, they shoot arrows and throw spears at the ships. I grab the hem of Marco's tunic and tug him toward the hatch. But he will not leave Pigafetta, who is calling down to the natives, trying to find the right words to stop the fighting.

Suddenly more canoes skim across the water toward the ships. This time they are not carrying spears, but baskets of food. They hold them high as if to say, "We bring gifts this time, not weapons." I lick my lips when I spy silver-finned fish and colorful fruit.

The sailors, who are more interested in eating than fighting, quickly drop their weapons. Magellan orders glass beads to be brought on deck. Quickly the beads are exchanged for food. Starving, we fall on the food like wolves. Only Espinosa continues to stalk from stern to bow, sword thrust before him.

While we are eating, the natives cut the line on the longboat and steal away with it. Espinosa shouts the alarm.

"Forty men!" Magellan calls out. "I command forty able crewmembers to suit up in armor. Take up your crossbows and swords. We will show these natives that the men of Spain and Portugal are all-powerful."

"Captain General, please do not resort to force," Pigafetta pleads. "You perceive these natives as threats, but haven't they also shared their own food?"

"Hush, worthless scholar." Espinosa pushes Pigafetta aside. "Captain General Magellan is correct. In the name of King Charles, we must conquer this island of thieves."

"We will show them the power of European weapons." Magellan straps on his sword.

Enrique brings Magellan his coat of mail, breastplate, and plumed helmet. The apprentice sailors carry spears and armor from the hold. Soon a small army is ready for battle.

I have never seen Magellan and the others in armor. They appear as clanging, frightening, mythical creatures.

Cannons boom on the *Trinidad*, sending a message

to the other ships in the armada. The longboats from the *Concepción* and *Victoria* arrive to pick up Magellan and the other soldiers. We watch as the boats land on shore. The *indios* stand, not raising their spears, simply staring.

I hear Magellan shout and the soldiers shoot their crossbows. One by one, the natives fall to the sand. Only after several have died do the others flee into the woods.

Magellan waves his arms and several soldiers set fire to the native's canoes. Then he leads a group

after the fleeing men. Soon we see smoke rising from the woods.

Marco gasps. "Has the captain general set their homes on fire too?"

Pigafetta's face is white. "I do not know, *niño.*"

Finally Magellan struts from the woods. The men march behind him, carrying yams, bananas, and chickens. We watch as they cut a cross and drive it into the sand. The soldiers fall to their knees and pray. Then they retrieve the stolen longboat, which they pile high with their plunder.

As the boats return to the ships, the native women slowly come on to the beach. They crouch next to the fallen and their wails reach us across the bay.

When Magellan and the rest are safely onboard, he raises his sword in triumph. "For our Almighty God and for King Charles, we have vanquished the warring natives."

Pigafetta sinks onto the deck of the ship. He blows his nose. "This should not have happened," he moans.

"But *signore*, the *indios* stole the captain general's boat," Marco says.

Pigafetta raises woeful eyes and I lie down next to him. "And for that they killed dozens and destroyed a village?"

Marco sighs. "It does not seem at all gallant or courageous."

"Nor is it. The captain general has named this place *Isla de los Ladrones*—the Isle of Thieves. If that is true, then we should be named the Ship of Thieves."

Pigafetta strokes my head. For once I do not shy from his touch. I am no stranger to death. Disease and accidents follow every voyage like dark clouds. But today's violence is new to me, and the cries of the women on the beach make me tremble.

I hope that Magellan is not becoming another Espinosa.

CHAPTER 11

Searching for the Spice Islands

March–April 1521

Once again the three ships plunge into the western sea, still in search of the Spice Islands. Fresh water and fruit have restored some of the sailors. Only one more dies, and the crew is solemn as his body is set adrift.

It isn't long before the *Trinidad* discovers another cluster of islands. Some have craggy cliffs; others are barren. Joyous voices sing out each time a new one is spotted. The crew is as hungry as I am to escape the close quarters of the stinking ship.

"These islands are not on any map," Pigafetta

tells Marco. "They remind me of what we Italians call the *arcipelago* of the Aegean Sea."

To our delight, Magellan finally orders the armada to drop anchor in a protected harbor and we take the longboat to shore. Boats from the *Concepción* and *Victoria* accompany us, and when we reach shore our spirits are high. A dense forest of palms rises beyond the beach, and my nose drinks in the scent of decaying leaves and fresh water.

Magellan orders that the Spanish flag and a cross be planted in the sand. "These islands are uncharted. We are the first to claim them in the name of King Charles and our Almighty God!"

The sailors fan out to hunt. I lead the way, lunging at rustles in the thick brush. I flush several birds and then a boar. The boar charges me, but I dart away, leading it toward the men.

After they kill it, they holler, "Leo the fierce hunter!" Even Espinosa gives me a reluctant nod. Later, I strut from the forest in front of the parade carrying the gutted animal.

Soon a fire is crackling and the boar is roasting. Marco and the other pages erect tents of sailcloth. No one wants to go back to the ship.

Our idyllic day is broken when I spot a canoe coming toward us. It is filled with brown-skinned men who row strongly. I bark, warning the crew.

Magellan orders the sailors to take up their weapons. "Do not make a move unless it is on my command," he tells them.

I watch alertly as the boat approaches and the natives climb out and wade to shore. A tall *indio*, bare chested with a cape of feathers around his neck, waves his arm. *"Homonhon,"* he declares, pointing at the trees. Then he holds out a basket of brown balls. *"Cocho."*

Pigafetta steps forward, bows, and takes the basket. "Thank you."

I sniff one of the brown *cochos*, but the hard-shelled fruit is not interesting. One of the natives raises a gleaming machete, and the sailors grip their weapons. But the *indio* brings the blade down hard on the *cocho*, slicing it in half. Milk spills out. He then cuts it in chunks and shows us how to pry the white flesh from the brown shell. I snatch up my own piece; the meat is nutty and sweet, and even to a dog it tastes delicious.

Enrique grins as he eats. "I remember these *cochos*. We must be getting close to my home."

Before rowing away, the natives use hand gestures that Pigafetta interprets as promising to bring more food. We carry *cochos* and boar to the sick sailors on board the *Trinidad*. The meat and milk seems to revive them, and after several days anchored on Homonhon, the entire crew is refreshed and ready to set out.

❧

The three ships weave their way around the many islands that Magellan names as a group *Las Islas de san Lazaro* for Saint Lazarus. We encounter more friendly natives willing to share their food. Finally our bellies are full, and as we continue through the maze of small islands, the once doubtful crew is eager to find the riches of the Moluccas.

As we travel, Pigafetta writes furiously in his journal, drawing pictures and noting details of the new foods and people we encounter. He talks out loud as he works and often Marco and I sit by his side, listening.

One night Pigafetta takes rare time away from his writing to fish. Marco is high in the mast, helping untangle a sail, so I alone help Pigafetta. He hums as he leans over the rail, pulling up the line, and I lick my lips, hoping he will land a fat fish. But the line catches.

"Diego will be angry if I break his line," Pigafetta tells me. "I'd better untangle it." Carefully he climbs over the railing and steps on a yard sticking over the side. I hear a scuffle, a scream, and then a splash as he slips off the pole and falls into the water.

Lusty cries come from below, so I know he is all right. But I cannot dive in after him. I race to the cookfire, but Enrique only pushes me away with his stick. I leap up the ladder to the quarterdeck. Diego is at the wheel. Grabbing his raggedy trouser leg, I tug. Then I whirl and race back to the leeward railing, barking.

Frowning, Diego stares and murmurs, "Crazy dog." Then he must hear Pigafetta's faint cry. "Grab the wheel!" he calls to the pilot, and then rushes with me to the railing. Pigafetta is below, arms flailing; the ship is swiftly leaving him behind.

Diego finds Beast, and the two lower a skiff into the water. I watch, trembling, as they row to Pigafetta and drag him into the small boat. A crowd gathers and their excited voices bring Marco down from the mast. He brings the *signore* a blanket.

Fortunately the island breezes and seawater are warm, and Pigafetta is not hurt. When he is safe on deck, he wraps me in his arms. "*Gracias*, Leo! You are proving to be a most worthy dog!"

Night falls. Pigafetta retires to his cabin early to change into dry clothes. Marco has the first watch

and I go with him. All evening sailors come up, grinning and calling me "Leo the *Héroe*." I squirm away from their attention, until finally dark envelops the ship and all is quiet.

Marco's eyes droop and he nods off. As the armada approaches another island, I spot the red glow of campfires along the dusky shores. I nudge him awake with my nose and together we wake Espinosa, who hurries to Magellan's cabin. A village has been sighted.

When the sun rises, a canoe bearing eight warriors speeds toward us.

Magellan greets them. This time Enrique understands their language. He is so delighted, he picks me up and dances around with me. Then he interprets for his master. The island is Limasawa, and the ruler, Rajah Kolambu, is eager to trade with us.

Pigafetta, Enrique (who will serve as interpreter), and Marco travel to the island to meet Kolambu and to send Magellan's regards. They take me along as well. "For protection," Pigafetta says, and I puff out my chest in pride.

As we slice through the water in the longboat, I stand tall, my paws propped on the bow. No longer am I the lowly rat dog. I have become hunter, savior, *and* protector. Not only have I forgotten to stay clear of humans, I have put myself right in the middle of them and their troubles.

Their praise has gone to my head.

Soon I will regret it.

CHAPTER 12

The Islands of Limasawa, Mactan, and Cebu

April 1521

Rajah Kolambu greets us with hands raised toward the sky. He has long black hair to his shoulders, wears earrings of gold, and carries a dagger in a carved scabbard. His body is bare to the waist and covered with tattoos. He invites Enrique and Pigafetta to share a feast, and I can sense the relief in both men that they are being well received.

Pigafetta is fascinated with the natives and the luxury of their village. Gold is everywhere—in jewelry, goblets, and dishes.

I am more fascinated with the island dogs that slink close to catch a sniff. I have not seen other dogs for many moons, and I growl at them to stay away. I have been in the company of men for too long and do not want these mongrels' friendships.

Enrique and Pigafetta sit on mats in a hut thatched with banana and palm leaves. Marco and I sit on the ground behind them. While we eat, Pigafetta shares his love of words with the natives. He has been practicing the language with Enrique, and he coaxes the Rajah to name objects at the table, which he repeats in their language and then writes on parchment.

Suddenly Kolambu reaches down, picks me up, and holds me high in the air. For a second, I am too startled to react. The Rajah gestures to Pigafetta to write down the word for me. I begin to squirm, wondering if the natives eat their dogs.

"That is Leo," Pigafetta states as he also writes "Leo the Hero" and points to me, still hanging in the air. Kolambu gives me a stiff pat and then sets

me next to Marco. The boy's eyes are wide, as if he too was worried I might join the stuffed chicken on the platter.

Kolambu is agreeable to supplying food for the ships' crews, and after the feast Pigafetta declares that the captain of the *Trinidad* has invited the Rajah to visit the ship.

We row back in the longboat with Rajah Kolambu

and several natives, who row in canoes. They bear gifts for Magellan.

On board the *Trinidad*, Magellan and Kolambu embrace and vow to be *casicasi*—blood brothers. The islanders trade rice and *orades*, a type of fish, for silk cloth and beads. Magellan shows them around the ship, boasting about traveling across the globe using compass and sea charts.

To impress the natives as well as demonstrate his power, Magellan has one of his gunners fire an *arquebus*, a long rifle. Then he has another man dress in breastplate, shield, helmet, and visor. Espinosa strikes the armored man with daggers and swords. Marco and the *indios* stare in openmouthed wonder at the mock fight, but I cringe at the loud clangs of steel on metal.

Espinosa continues to hit the soldier with all his might, but he does not fall. Magellan puffs out his chest. "One of these armed men is worth a hundred of yours," he tells Kolambu.

The Rajah wisely agrees.

"Sunday will be Easter, the day our people worship our God and his son," Magellan tells Kolambu. "The officers and crew from all the ships will land on the beach to celebrate mass. I entreat the Limasawans to worship the rising of Christ with us."

On Sunday the islanders eagerly join in the Easter ceremony. They fall on their knees and raise clasped hands to the cross. Muskets fire on shore and loud blasts respond from the ships. The village dogs cower at the noise, so I pretend the booms do not bother me.

We feast again, my favorite part. The natives are generous with their food and wine. Because they are curious about me—"Leo the Hero"—they poke my ribs. They inspect my teeth, paws, and tail. They also slip me bites of peppered goat and ginger-spiced fish, so I do not mind their inspections.

After the feast, Magellan has several of his soldiers fence with single-handed swords to further impress the Limasawans.

"Rajah Kolambu, do you have any enemies?" Magellan asks. As always, Enrique interprets the words of the two leaders. Pigafetta listens as well, trying to learn the language.

"Yes, there are two islands hostile to the Limasawans," Kolambu replies. "Mactan and Cebu. We trade with Cebu, so the Cebuans may not cause us problems."

Magellan raises his own sword. "We will go with our ships and make these people obedient to you, Rajah Kolambu, and to our Spanish ruler, King Charles."

Kolambu seems pleased with the idea. Blood brothers with Magellan, he volunteers to act as pilot when we go to find these enemies.

❧

The next day, on board the *Trinidad*, Rajah Kolambu directs the three ships to sail into a channel between Mactan and Cebu, but to land at Cebu. Villages dot the palm-shaded shores of the island. The houses are built on stilts, their sides and roofs thatched with leaves.

"Do you think this was your home?" Marco asks Enrique.

"I do not know," Enrique says. "But it seems like paradise to me."

"Unfurl the banners! Fire a greeting!" Magellan orders when we anchor in the bay.

The cannons thunder across the water. We watch as the Cebuans scatter from the beach, frightened by the booming mortars.

"Our firepower has impressed these *indios*," Magellan tells Kolambu. "We will easily conquer and claim this island for Spain."

"King Humabon of Cebu can be benevolent. Still, it is custom for all ships entering his port to pay tribute to the great ruler," Kolambu warns.

Magellan shakes his head. "King Charles of Spain is the only great ruler in the world," he says.

"The Armada de Molucca will never pay tribute to a lesser king like Humabon. If the Cebuan king wishes war, then he will have war."

I hear the fiery tone in Magellan's voice, and I stand proudly beside him. Am I not a hunter and protector too?

Humabon must be impressed by the firepower of the three ships, because when he arrives by canoe, he bears gifts for Magellan. "I will pay tribute to your captain and this powerful king of Spain," he tells all of us on the *Trinidad*. "We have brought a great feast to your ships."

In return, Magellan trades glass beads, bolts of fine linen, and gilt drinking cups. With Enrique interpreting, Pigafetta records the natives' language. Like the Limasawans, the Cebuans are thrilled to see their words on paper.

Days later we are in Pigafetta's cabin. I am under the small table, chewing a bone left over from one of the many feasts the Cebuans have prepared for us. Marco is reading over the scribe's shoulder as he writes in his journal:

Man: *lac*. Woman: *perampuan*. Gold: *boloan*. Silver: *pilla*. Pepper: *malissa*. Cloves: *chiande*. Cinnamon: *manna*.

"Where *are* the *malissa*, *chiande*, and *manna*?" Marco asks. "If we were in the Spice Islands, we would have discovered them by now."

Pigafetta smiles. "I see you are learning the language too."

"It has been easy since we have been anchored by Cebu for over a week," Marco says. "And you have done nothing but record words. Why are we not on our way to the Moluccas?"

"I am not sure, but it appears our leader wants to show the islanders the superiority of our arms and our King." Pigafetta closes his journal. "And it also appears that Magellan is growing more spiritual. He wants to continue to introduce the Cebuans to our God so they worship him instead of their god, an idol with tusks like a pig."

Marco shrugs. "Their idols have brought the Cebuans more riches than heaven could ever bestow on them."

"Hush, *niño*," Pigafetta says as he glances toward the cabin door. "Do not let Magellan hear such blasphemous talk. King Humabon and Rajah Kolambu wish to be baptized, and it is making Magellan feverish with joy. The captain general will order the armada's departure when he is ready. Until then, enjoy the island's bounty—like Leo our friend here, who is gnawing this fine bone. Soon enough we will again be eating wormy hardtack."

On the day of the baptismal ceremony, Pigafetta, Enrique, Marco, and I accompany Magellan, a priest, and forty seamen to Cebu. Cannons boom from the ships as we approach the shore in our longboats, a royal banner waving.

A wooden platform has been built in the village. It is adorned with palm branches and flowers. The *Trinidad*'s priest performs the baptismal ceremony. Humabon takes the name Charles; Kolambu takes the name John. To celebrate being "brothers of the same faith," Magellan again has the ships fire their artillery.

Then all the natives are in a frenzy to be baptized. I do not understand these ceremonies of sprinkling water and bowing before crosses. Instead I chase the village goats and pigs, while keeping Marco and Pigafetta in sight. I trot back as soon as the feasting begins. Pigafetta sits near Magellan to translate.

"Now that you are a Christian, you will conquer your enemies," Magellan declares.

"That will not be so easy," Humabon says. "The chieftains of Mactan—Sulu and Lapu Lapu—resist my rule."

Magellan slams down his mug, making me jump. "They must obey you as King Humabon, now christened Charles, and swear allegiance to Spain, or we will kill them and give their land to you."

Humabon cocks his head. "This is my new God's will?"

Magellan nods emphatically. "He wishes us to show the heathens who worship idols that our faith and our Spanish king will be victorious."

Suddenly fierce screeching comes from the sky and a large black bird swoops into the hut. I leap from under the table, snapping as the bird dips and rises over the platters of food. It caws loudly as if shouting a warning. The islanders and sailors grow silent and even Magellan stops boasting to cross his chest.

"A bird of ill omen," Pigafetta murmurs. "The Italians believe that a bird entering your house foretells death." Dropping his hand, he reaches for me, and I scoot beside him so his fingers can dig into my ruff.

The bird soars from the hut as swiftly as it came. Trembling, I watch it disappear.

CHAPTER 13

Mactan

April 1521

To make good on his threat, Magellan sends a band of men across the channel to Mactan. They set fire to a village whose inhabitants refuse to obey King Humabon. Before leaving, the soldiers pound a large wooden cross into the ground.

King Sulu of Mactan brings Magellan a peace offering of two goats. I nip at their hocks as they mill on the deck of the *Trinidad*. They lower their heads to butt me, but I scamper out of reach.

"I would have sent more," Sulu explains as Pigafetta translates to Magellan, "but Lapu Lapu, who shares the island, will not bend to the will of the

Spanish. You burned one of his villages to the ground and he is angry."

"He will not convert to Christianity?" Magellan asks.

Sulu shakes his head. "Not without war. My soldiers are at your service to fight him," he offers.

"Thank you, but we need no help. The Spanish lions will show these islanders how to win." With those words, our leader declares war on King Lapu Lapu of Mactan.

After Sulu leaves and Magellan goes into his cabin, the sailors whisper their fears. "If the crew is lost in battle, what will we do? Will we live on the islands as Cebuans? Will we ever see Spain again?"

Marco throws an arm around me. "Magellan believes that the natives will flee without a fight. But he has made the Mactans angry with his demands. What if they kill us? I do not want to die so young."

His grip grows tighter, and I wiggle away from him. Troubles are coming too thick and fast for this sea dog, and I find a rat to chase.

Magellan has summoned the officers from the other ships to discuss his declaration of war. Soon they arrive in their longboats. Pigafetta joins Espinosa, Captain Serrano from the *Concepción,* Captain Barbosa from the *Victoria,* and the other officers on the forecastle. The rest of the crew, while pretending to work, keep eyes and ears on the meeting.

Serrano speaks the loudest. "We cannot wage war on the islanders," he protests. "Converting the natives to Christianity was a fine mission, but we were sent to find the Spice Islands."

"Those were our orders from King Charles," a pilot agrees. "Why are we continuing to be anchored here? Why are we inserting ourselves in the islanders' problems?"

"With all due respect, Captain General, I agree with these men," Pigafetta says. "Do not take drastic measures against Lapu Lapu. We can solve this disagreement in a peaceful manner."

Barbosa adds his own warning: "We have already suffered casualties from disease. We have lost two

121

ships. Gathering a force large enough to fight the Mactans means more losses."

"It also means our ships will be nearly empty and open to attack," Serrano says.

As the men argue, Magellan paces the length of the forecastle, almost stepping on my tail. Finally he stops and faces them. "I hear your concerns," he says. "We will reduce the number of our fighters, and keep the ships far from shore so they cannot be attacked. However, I have no doubt that we *will* be victorious against the Mactans. It is God's plan."

Serrano bows. "Then we will leave you in the hands of the Lord, Captain General. Our place is with the ships." With those words, he stalks off, the officers of the other ships behind him.

Pigafetta remains. I see despair etched in his face, but he too bows and says, "I will stand with you, Captain General."

"As I will," Espinosa echoes.

The next day, Magellan orders the crew to prepare for battle. I want to hide below deck, but I cannot run from these men I have lived with for so long. I pace around the gunners and sailors as they don armor and turn into warriors. Several rub my back for good luck. Diego and Beast pat me solemnly, as if it is the last time.

As Marco helps Pigafetta with his armor, he entreats him not to go. "You are a scholar, not a fighter," he declares as he straps gauntlets onto his wrists.

"I will be well armed, with sixty brave men and our valiant leader," Pigafetta says.

"Do you know how to wield a sword and jab a lance?" Marco asks. Taking his master's worn velvet hat, he replaces it with a hard helmet.

"Well enough," Pigafetta says quietly.

"But have you *killed* a man?" When Pigafetta does not reply, Marco sighs and looks down at me. "You must take Leo with you, then. He has been our savior many times. Perhaps he will make sure you return safely to the *Trinidad.*"

Pigafetta bends over and rests his hand on my

head. It is weighed down by the metal glove. I see the sadness in his face as if he knows this battle will be lost. Placing my paws on his knee, I whine to let him know that I will go with him. Did he not name me Leo the Brave?

Before dawn the next day, we arrive off the shores of Mactan in twenty Cebuan boats. Magellan has ordered the *Trinidad, Concepción,* and *Victoria* to anchor far from the battle. He has instructed the Cebuans not to fight, but instead to observe the power of Spanish weapons and warriors.

The sea air is thick with worry and fear, and a huge sigh fills the boat when Magellan once more offers the Mactans a peaceful solution.

"Send this message to King Lapu Lapu," Magellan tells Humabon. "If his people obey the king of Spain, recognize the Christian king, and pay us tribute, then we will be his friend. If not, he will see how the Spanish lions fight."

Humabon sends a messenger in a canoe to the island. As the sun rises, the *indio* returns with a reply from Lapu Lapu. "Our weapons are strong, our lances made from stout bamboo, our stakes hardened with fire. We will not bend to the rule of Spain."

Magellan stands tall in the rocking longboat. "We will fight then," he declares. "We will show Lapu Lapu the strength of *our* warriors."

Magellan waves the men forward. Pigafetta jumps into the surf. In one hand he holds his sword. In the other, he holds me as he and the seamen wade awkwardly toward the shore. The water is waist high and their movements are ponderous due to their heavy armor.

When it is shallow enough for the waves to break, I leap from Pigafetta's arms. Sand and surf splash into my face as I follow the men, so it is hard to see. But I hear the fierce whoops of natives, and before we reach the beach, the Mactans charge from the trees.

"Two divisions!" Magellan hollers. "Crossbows front right! Musketeers front left!"

The natives hurl bamboo spears. Pigafetta's armor repels several sharp-pointed arrows. Beside him,

Espinosa and a line of gunners shoot into the throng. But the natives leap and dance, and most shots miss.

"Burn the village!" Magellan cries when the Mactans retreat into the woods. We advance toward a palm grove. The huts seem deserted. I prick my ears, listening. It is silent.

Torches are lighted and houses are set on fire. As the flames leap into the sky, the Mactans, armed with swords and leather shields, fall upon us from all sides.

We are trapped and outnumbered.

"Retreat!" Magellan cries.

Gunners and sailors scatter. Diego and Beast give final thrusts of their swords and then race for the beach.

I bark at Pigafetta to leave. He is standing by Magellan's side, along with Espinosa and several others.

Suddenly a warrior races toward them with an upraised knife. I bark again, and Pigafetta turns in time to fend off the attack with his round shield.

The Mactans keep coming in droves. One shoots Magellan in the leg with an arrow. Another hurls a spear into his face. A third knocks off his helmet. Still another thrusts a bamboo spear at his arm.

I sink my teeth into bare ankles. Magellan strikes with his lance. But nothing seems to stop the attackers.

"Retreat! Retreat!" Magellan tries to draw his sword, but the wound in his arm has weakened him. A Mactan charges him with outstretched dagger. Whirling, I leap for the native's wrist. A knife slices my leg, and I fall to the ground. Feet stomp and kick me and I roll from the melee.

There are too many warriors to fight.

I spy Pigafetta, who is slashing right and left with his sword. Blood has pooled under his eye from a cut on his forehead. Grabbing the back of his stocking, I pull him toward the beach. He plunges into the surf, following the other fleeing soldiers.

I bound after him, my slashed leg bleeding. It is hard to paddle and I feel myself falling behind. Suddenly I am scooped up in a strong arm.

Espinosa presses me against his corselet. "We cannot lose you now, Leo the Brave," he says.

As Espinosa surges through the surf, I glance back over his shoulder. The Mactans are hurling themselves upon Magellan, and he disappears in a hail of blows.

He is dying, and there is nothing I can do.

CHAPTER 14

Cebu

May 1521

I t is several days after the battle, and the crew is still shaken. Espinosa gives commands in a low voice. Gunners clean weapons in silence. Hernando bustles from sailor to sailor, patching wounds.

The officers have voted on new captains. Serrano and Barbosa will share leadership of the *Trinidad*. Luis Alfonso de Gois will be the *Victoria's* new captain. Juan Elcano takes over as master of the *Concepción*. It is also decided that as soon as the ships are ready, we will depart Cebu.

Pigafetta sits on a crate on the deck of the *Trinidad*, his forehead swollen to twice its usual size. Marco dabs his cut with a rag soaked in seawater. "Your wound is foul." He wrinkles his nose.

"It is from the poisons in the Mactan arrow," Pigafetta says. "That, and the jab of too many spears, is what felled Magellan as well."

"And the reluctance of the other officers to come to your aid," Marco says in a low voice. "Eight of our men killed, including our leader. Those deaths could have been prevented if the *Trinidad* had fired its cannons onto the beach."

Pigafetta hushes him. "You are speaking of treason, which cannot be proven. And when our ships did fire, they were too far off shore to be effective."

"Not treason, then. But the other captains have long spoken of getting rid of the captain general. Look how quickly Barbosa and Serrano were voted to be the *Trinidad*'s new leaders." Rinsing the rag, Marco frowns at the cut. "The barber needs to make a poultice of marjoram."

"Time will heal me," Pigafetta says. "Hernando has his hands full with the others."

Marco bends to wash my leg. It is not a large gash. I have licked it clean, and Hernando rubbed it with salve when no one was looking. Still, the salt stings and I whimper.

"Be brave, my hero," Marco says.

Espinosa comes over to us. The thud of his boots on the deck no longer sends shivers down my spine. He does not admit to saving me, but he does not call me *cao sujo* anymore.

"Bad news, *signore*," he says to Pigafetta. He looks as weary as the rest of the crew. "We have tried to negotiate, but Lapu Lapu refused to release the remains of the fallen soldiers. His messenger said the king will not give Magellan's body or armor to us for all the riches in the world."

The news brings tears to Pigafetta's eyes. Espinosa bows to show support of his grief and then leaves.

"Magellan will not receive a Christian burial," Pigafetta says sadly. "Though no one else on the ships seems to care. The officers and crew do not mourn his death nor feel the need for a proper service. They felt our captain general's thirst for glory led to his and the others' deaths. Only Enrique feels the loss."

Marco snorts. "Enrique has taken to his bed, yes. But it is not because of sadness for Magellan. Captains Serrano and Barbosa have refused to honor his freedom." Leaning closer, the page adds, "Enrique has confided that he will have his revenge."

Pigafetta rises abruptly. "I hope not. These ships have seen enough sorrow."

Loud voices reach us from the forecastle. I look up to see Serrano and Enrique arguing.

"I will no longer follow orders!" Enrique declares. "You are not my master."

"You will stay with the ship as an interpreter," Serrano says. "You are still a slave and you will be whipped if you do not obey."

"Magellan freed me with his death, so I am a slave no longer." Furious, Enrique swiftly climbs on top of a yard and jumps into the water.

Marco, Pigafetta, and I rush to look over the railing. With strong strokes Enrique swims to a nearby Cebuan fishing canoe and climbs in.

"Is he leaving us?" Marco asks in a shocked voice.

"I would not be surprised. Knowing the language, he has befriended many on the island."

Marco heaves a sigh. "And he has often expressed his wish for freedom. Captain Serrano should not have insisted he stay a slave."

"I agree." Pigafetta shakes his head. "Magellan may have been misguided in his quest once he reached these islands," he tells Marco. "But this new conflict is proof that our small armada will be lost without his guidance."

I bark after Enrique as he rows away with the Cebuan fisherman, but he only stiffens his shoulders and does not turn his head.

Days later, supplies are loaded and we are ready to depart. There is still no word of Enrique. Marco laments that his friend has left us for good. Pigafetta feels that Enrique has somehow found his real home and will not miss us.

As we are preparing the ship to leave, a messenger arrives in a canoe. King Humabon wants to honor the Spanish lions with one last feast.

The crew and officers accept.

"I cannot go," Pigafetta says. Not only is his forehead swollen, but one eye is halfway shut.

Marco chooses to stay behind with him. Though I usually love a good feast, I am happy to stay onboard, far from the crush of humans.

The ship is blissfully quiet. Pigafetta writes in his journal. Marco reads his master's tattered copy of *The Iliad*.

Rested, I patrol the boat, though I am still limping. Baskets of cochas and fruit fill the hull. Salted fish are packed in barrels. Fresh tar coats walls, decks, and riggings. Sturdy wood planks have replaced wormy ones. The new captains are eager to reach the Spice Islands, and all seems to be ready.

Sniffing, I check for *bichos* that have snuck aboard. My joints feel creaky and I wince with each step. The battle took its toll on me as well, and I am no longer a pup. For truth, my days as hunter and protector are waning. Hopefully I can still serve my ship as a ratter.

Sudden shouting brings me running to the top deck. Espinosa is climbing over the railing from the rope ladder dropped to one of the longboats. He is followed by the pilot Albo and a few other men. Pigafetta's face is ashen, and I can tell that something is terribly wrong.

"The invitation for a feast was a trap!" Espinosa exclaims. "Set by King Humabon and Enrique."

"A trap? I-I don't understand," Pigafetta stutters.

"We were attacked by armed Cebuan warriors," Espinosa explains breathlessly. "Enrique convinced Humabon that the only way to appease Lapu Lapu of Mactan was to become an enemy of Spain. The

Cebuans are angry at Humabon for his loyalty to Magellan and they turned on us."

"What about the others who went to the feast?" Pigafetta asks.

Albo shakes his head "Captains Barbosa and Serrano—dead. We must raise the anchor, sail closer, and fire onto the shore. Perhaps we can save the rest."

The men quickly assemble the crew and the gunners. Pigafetta stays frozen by the railing.

"Enrique did this?" Marco whispers.

Pigafetta's shoulders slump in reply.

Cries from the water make us look down. I poke my head through the railing and see several sailors swimming to the ship. On the beach, flames rise into the sky, arrows dart through the air, and people drop lifeless on the sand.

I bark to alert Pigafetta and Marco, who lower more ladders and help the swimmers climb on board. One of them is Beast.

"The Cebuans are coming to massacre us all," he says. "Other men are swimming to the *Victoria* and *Concepción* to warn them as well. We must set sail now!"

Espinosa takes charge. After all this time at sea, the crew needs little direction. Two apprentices scamper up the foremast, ready to unfurl the sail. Others push the capstan and pull up the anchor rope. Climbing a shroud, Marco jumps onto a rigging above my head and swings like a monkey before making his way up the mainmast.

"Ease the rope of the foresail and with God's speed let us leave this cursed island!" Espinosa hollers.

Cannons fire mortar onto the beach, but it is not slowing the frenzy of the *indios*. They jump into their canoes and by the time the ships are turned, they have reached the *Trinidad*.

Espinosa orders the musketeers to fire, and sharp pops ring through the air. For once I am glad for his fierce commands and our weapons' sharp retorts.

The *Trinidad* heads for the open ocean; the *Victoria* and *Concepción* are right behind. The sails fill with wind and our speed picks up. The canoes keep aside us, but the natives' spears and arrows cannot reach the top deck.

Pigafetta ignores the fiery gun blasts, the shouting officers, and the rushing crew. Slowly he picks up his journal and walks to the leeward side of the ship. His stride is sluggish and his shoulders are still slumped.

"Enrique betrayed us, Leo," he murmurs. "He had reason to be angry at Captain Serrano, but not at those who called him friend. Now the Cebuans who fought by our side have turned against us. Officers and crew have been killed. What more can we face?"

Crouching beside me, he points behind us toward shore, where a tower of flames rises into the sky. "Look on the hill. The natives are burning our cross. Magellan's desire to turn the Cebuans into Christians failed. His fight against Lapu Lapu failed." He heaves a sigh, and I lick his hand, hoping to erase the forlorn look on his face.

Suddenly Marco swings from a shroud and lands

with a thump on the deck, startling us both. *"Signore,"* he exclaims. "Why the long face? We are finally bound for the Spice Islands as we have wished!"

"Except we have left the fallen behind and are pursued by murderers," Pigafetta declares.

"That is true, master, and many have been killed. But we must stop looking backward. Look forward!" He waves toward the blue sky and the unbroken horizon past the bow. Pigafetta stands and stares at the scene. I plant my feet on the railing, looking too. "Treasures await." Marco throws his arms wide. "Gold, spices, new adventures!"

"Only, Magellan will not be with us," Pigafetta says dejectedly. "And his past discoveries will be forgotten—finding the strait, crossing the western sea, claiming new islands. He led us where no one else has dared to travel and now he is gone."

"No, *signore*, he will not be forgotten." Marco slips the journal from Pigafetta's grasp and flips it open. "You have recorded everything. When we return to

Spain, you will tell King Charles and his court the true story of our courageous captain general."

Pigafetta's eyes grow wide. "Why, you are right, *niño*. Though perhaps I cannot call you *niño* anymore. Not only have you proven to be a wise counsel, but under Diego and Beast's tutelage, you have turned into an able seaman."

Marco grins. "And you, noble scholar, have proven yourself to be a brave warrior."

"With Leo's help," Pigafetta says as he pats me on the head.

"Yes, Leo has shown again and again that he is indeed brave."

"Perhaps I need to devote several entries in my journal to the ship's remarkable dog."

I know they are talking about me, so I scratch an ear to feign my disinterest.

"It would be more uplifting than writing about Magellan's death and Enrique's betrayal. Remember how Leo saved me from Espinosa and the storm?"

Marco stoops and slips his arms around my ribs and picks me up. "The king should know about our brave sea dog. We would not have survived this journey without your loyalty, Leo."

This time I do not squirm to be put down. I lean against Marco's chest, enjoying the warmth of his touch and the thump of his heart.

Loyalty. It is a new word for me. It has taken me two oceans to trust these two humans and to learn

that loyalty does not mean duty or obedience. It means caring for someone and standing by him as a friend.

Marco, Pigafetta, and I have survived storms, hunger, disease, treachery, and the deaths of many members of our crew. I had to travel halfway around the world to learn that whatever perils befall us, we can face them together—and survive.

As the *Trinidad* cuts through the waves, leaving the pursuing natives far behind, the three of us stare past the bowsprit to the vast ocean beyond. Will we make it around the world as Captain General Magellan once hoped? I do not know. But as my friend Marco said, it is time to look forward.

And so I do. The wind flaps my ears and once again I wonder at the adventures ahead. Despite all we have endured, it feels as if the voyage is just beginning.

The History Behind *Leo*

Author's Note

The true story of Magellan, his officers and crew, and their journey around the world is incredibly complex politically, culturally, ethically, socially, historically, and morally. *Over the Edge of the World: Magellan's Terrifying Circumnavigation of the Globe,* by Laurence Bergreen, is an in-depth and carefully researched book about the voyage. It is 414 pages, including fifteen pages of notes on sources and a nine-page bibliography.

Leo, Dog of the Sea is a fictional story of the journey, told through the eyes of a seaworthy dog. Any factual and historical discrepancies in the book are mine—and Leo's.

The Rest of the Story

At the end of *Leo, Dog of the Sea,* Marco, Leo, and Pigafetta escape the island of Cebu (now part of the Philippines) and sail hopefully toward the Moluccas, also known as the Spice Islands (now called the Malukas, part of Indonesia). In reality, the remaining ships were far from reaching their destination.

Only 107 members of the original crew of 270 remained. The *Concepíon* was rotten, the wood hull damaged by tropical water worms, so it was burned. That left only the *Victoria* and *Trinidad,* which continued on, sailing blindly from island to island, the sailors looting and pirating to stay alive.

The crew finally spotted the island of Tidore on November 6, 1521. The survivors had found their destination. They packed the two ships with cinnamon, nutmeg, ginger, and cloves, as well as goats and chickens for the trip back to Spain.

But before they could leave, the *Trinidad's* hull split open. Gomez de Espinosa and a small crew were left behind on Tidore to repair it. The *Victoria*, with a crew of forty-seven men, departed for Spain.

On September 6, 1522, almost three years after the Armada de Moluccas had departed, the *Victoria* returned to Spain. The battered ship carried the pilot Francisco Albo, the barber Hernando Bustamente, the sailor Diego, a page named Juan, and Antonio Pigafetta, the learned man from Italy, as well as thirteen other survivors. The valiant *Victoria* and the last of its crew had traveled 40,777 miles.

Pigafetta published four copies of his journal, *The First Voyage around the World: An Account of Magellan's Expedition*. From his writings, today's readers can glimpse the wonders of discovering new cultures, ecosystems, and countries. His journal was also extremely helpful to me for researching and writing Leo and Marco's adventures.

Captain General Ferdinand Magellan's body was never recovered. Pigafetta wrote, "...more accurately than any man in the world did he navigate and make sea charts....and no other had had so much natural talent nor the boldness nor knowledge to sail around the world, as he had almost done" (page 62), but at the time, few believed these claims. According to Bergreen, "Ferdinand Magellan remains controversial even today, considered a tyrant, a traitor, a visionary, and a hero..." (page 415). Historians do recognize that he was the first European to navigate and map the Strait of Magellan (named long after his death) and the first to cross the Pacific Ocean, which he named Mar Pacifico, meaning peaceful sea.

About Leo

There are no records of a dog on board any of Magellan's ships. However, dogs have long been used in Spain to control mice and rats (and the armada's five ships were infested with both). Today there are five recognized "rat-hunting" breeds in Spain, including the Gos Rater Valencia and the Ratonero Bodeguero Andaluz, both similar to our hero Leo.

The first proof of a ship's dog dates to 1545. "Hatch" is called the "world's oldest sea dog" (Irvine). His skeleton was recovered by divers salvaging the English galleon *The Mary Rose*, which sank north of the Isle of Wright. His bones were found near the "hatch" of the carpenter's cabin, and the name stuck. It is thought that he was the ship's ratter and mascot. Today Hatch is one of the most popular exhibits at The Mary Rose Museum in Portsmouth, United Kingdom.

Officers and Crew

There were distinct levels of seamen on a ship. At the bottom were the lowly pages, boys eight to ten years old like Marco, who acted as servants. Many pages were orphans, roaming the beaches and streets before they were captured and forced to work on the ships. Fortunate pages had a protector like Pigafetta.

Others were ship's pages and ordered about by every-one else on the ship.

Apprentice sailors and sailors were ranked above the pages. On Magellan's voyage, these men were from almost every country. They communicated with each other by using a specialized language called "nautical Castilian." If a captain ordered, *"Iza el trinquete,"* all the sailors would understand that he meant "raise the foresail."

Seasoned sailors steered the ship, or as they said, "handled the helm." In order to steer, a sailor pushed down and either right or left on the whipstaff, a large piece of timber, which then turned the tiller, which moved the rudder. (A ship's wheel was not used in the 1500s. Historians believe it was

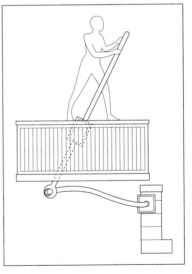

whipstaff

invented in the early 1700s.) While he steered, the sailor also had to have "his eyes fixed simultaneously on the compass and the position of the sails and ears attentive to the orders given him by the pilot..." (Perez-Mallaina *Ferdinand Magellan: Circumnavigating the World*, page 78).

Above the sailors were the officers, including the steward, the pilot, the master-in-arms, and—at the very top—the captain. The steward oversaw the ship's supplies. The pilot was responsible for navigation. This was no easy job, as his only tools were the stars and hand-drawn charts. The master-in-arms was the administrator and constable of the ship. The captain governed the entire ship, using Spanish maritime code (*Consulado del Mare*) to spell out the sailors' work, diet, and punishments. For example, the code stated that meat should be served three days a week. Punishment could include being "plunged into the sea with a rope from the yard arm three times..." (Bergreen, page 115).

Hardships of the Voyage

The men had to endure so many hardships that it is amazing any of them survived. Violent storms, freezing cold, withering heat, starvation, thirst, overcrowding, disease, punishing work, mutinies, and the fear of sailing into the unknown plagued them throughout the journey.

At the beginning of its journey, the armada encountered sixty days of rain. Pigafetta wrote, "...many furious squalls of wind, and currents of water struck us head on" (page 8). Storms continued to buffet the ships across the Atlantic and along the coast of South America. Once they entered the strait, the men experienced what Pigafetta termed a "great storm," which is now called a williwaw. Glaciers surrounding the strait chilled the air and sent it blasting down the mountains toward the water. This created winds so fierce and disorienting that the *San Antonio* and *Concepción* both became lost.

Often the ships were trapped in doldrums, drifting on calm water for weeks in stifling heat, with no wind to stir the sails. At the other extreme, they experienced strong gales and bitterly cold temperatures from February to August of 1520, the winter months in the southern hemisphere. "When the fleet reached latitude 45°S, the first blast from the Antarctic struck with ferocity. The seamen, in wet, icy clothes, suffered raw, stinging hands and feet. They feared freezing to death" (Levinson, *Magellan: And the First Voyage around the World,* page 62).

Conditions on the Ships

Brutal work was constant, food and water scarce, pests inescapable, and cleanliness and privacy unknown.

Ships were small—the *Trinidad* was approximately eighty feet in length, the *Victoria* was about sixty. (A football field is 360 feet long and today's ocean liners are usually over 1,000 feet.) Each ship was packed with people, supplies, and animals. After they had been at sea for a while, the ship became so dirty and smelly that it was known as a *"pajaro puerco,* a flying pig" (Bergreen, page 111).

Captains were the ultimate authority. Seamen not only were ordered to man the sails day and night, but they also had to venture ashore to find food and water, chop wood, repair the hull, mend the rigging, load and unload supplies, catch and cook food, work the bilge pump, and keep watch, no matter how fierce the weather. In many voyages, the sailors were also pressed into defense of their ships—and themselves.

The constant work was more difficult when food and water were scarce. As they crossed the Pacific, Pigafetta wrote, "We were three months and twenty days without getting any kind of fresh food. We ate biscuit...swarming with worms... We drank yellow water that had been putrid for many days" (page 26).

Without fresh food, sailors developed scurvy, a disease unknown at the time. Pigafetta describes the illness in his journal: "Nineteen men died from the sickness... However, I, by the grace of God, suffered no sickness" (page 27). It is now known that scurvy is caused by a lack of vitamin C, and historians have speculated that the officers' supplies of quince jelly, made from a fruit similar to a pear, may have saved Pigafetta and others from the disease.

The captain and his officers had small cabins on the ships, but sailors slept wherever they could find a dry spot. They curled up in the ropes and sails, and between barrels and crates. They were lucky if they had straw pallets and wool blankets stored in their sea chests, which were tied down on deck. Still, sleep was made even more difficult by the biting lice, cockroaches, and bedbugs that burrowed into hair and clothing, as well as the infestations of rats and mice.

Mutinies

Throughout the long voyage, Magellan had to remain alert for uprisings from the officers and crew. Magellan was Portuguese, but he sailed for the King of Spain. Most of his officers were Spanish and resented the Portuguese captain.

Not long after the armada departed Sanlúcar de Barrameda, Magellan received an urgent message from Spain from Diogo Barbosa, his father-in-law, notifying him that his life was in danger. Led by Juan de Cartagena, the captains of three of the ships were planning to mutiny and possibly kill Magellan.

In April 1520, another mutiny erupted at Port Saint Julian. Magellan discovered the treachery, foiled the revolt, and later brutally punished all who were involved. Luis de Mendoza, captain of the *Victoria,* was stabbed to death. Another traitor was beheaded, others were tortured, and many of them died from their injuries. Juan de Cartagena, captain of the *San Antonio,* was marooned on an island, and forty seamen were shackled and condemned to hard labor. "Magellan had succeeded in terrorizing all the men under his command, captains and commoners alike" (Bergreen, page 151).

Magellan had demonstrated his power, but he had also incurred his men's wrath. The officers and crew of the *San Antonio* continued to plot against him. Later, when Magellan ordered the *San Antonio* and *Concepción* to sail ahead and explore what later turned out to be the strait to the Pacific, the *San Antonio* did not return. The officers and crew had forced the ship's captain to return to Spain. Once there, the men declared that Magellan was a madman and was unfaithful to Spain. Both the king of Spain and the king of Portugal declared Magellan a traitor.

The Unknown

Before Magellan's voyage, Spanish and Portuguese mariners had explored the coast of South America and attempted to find a passage from the Atlantic Ocean to the Spice Islands. In the 1500s, Vasco Núñez de Balboa had sighted the Pacific Ocean (though it was not thus named), but had not reached it. Few of these explorers left behind maps, and those that were available were hand drawn and closely guarded. No one knew the vastness of the earth. When Magellan set out, he was basically sailing into the unknown.

Magellan and his pilots relied on several tools and strategies to find their way:

🪶 Quadrants and astrolabes, along with the stars, were used to identify latitude (the distance above and below the equator).

🪶 Nautical charts helped them locate coastlines and waterways.

🪶 Compasses and the polar star helped them identify their direction.

🪶 Lead lines—knotted ropes dropped into the water—measured depth and determined currents.

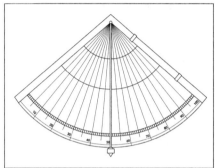

quadrant

astrolabe

None of these tools were totally accurate, and at the time of the voyage, longitude (the distance east and west around the earth) could not be measured. Considering these limitations, it is incredible that Magellan was able to steer a course almost all the way around the world.

Discovering New Cultures

King Charles of Spain had ordered Magellan to deal fairly with the natives he met on his journey, telling him, "You shall not cheat them in any way, and... You shall not consent in any manner that any wrong or harm be done to them..." (Bergreen, page 49). But the captain general and his men had mixed emotions about how to treat natives. They had heard stories about Juan de Solis, another explorer; he and seven of his crew were slain and eaten by a tribe during his exploration of South America.

The differences between European and native cultures were startling to the seamen. "These people are heathens," Pigafetta wrote about the natives of one of the islands now known as the Philippines. "They go naked and painted" (page 42).

Some encounters were successful. Magellan had brought many items to trade. In Brazil, the natives were eager to exchange fresh food for trinkets. "For one fishhook or one knife, those people gave us five or six chickens; for one comb, a pair of geese; for one mirror or one pair of scissors, as many fish as would be sufficient for ten men," Pigafetta wrote (page 9).

Trading for food throughout the long voyage saved the crew from starvation. The natives also provided navigational guidance, helping the *Victoria* and *Trinidad* finally find the Spice Islands.

Other encounters were disastrous. When Magellan reached the Philippines, he was discovering new territory. The islands were not on European maps. The natives had previously only encountered Arab and Chinese explorers. Magellan was interested in trade, but also intent on claiming new lands for Spain and converting the natives to Christianity. When this did not work, he and his crew resorted to firepower. Early in the voyage, when natives stole one of the longboats, "…the captain general in wrath went ashore with forty armed men, and they burned some forty and fifty houses together with many boats, killed seven men, and recovered the small boat" (Pigafetta, page 29).

This was not the only ruthless encounter between Europeans and natives. Magellan's zeal to thwart anyone who defied him caused him to send his men to the island of Mactan. Pigafetta wrote, "We burned one hamlet which was located on a neighboring island, because it refused to obey the king or us" (page 53). And of course, Magellan's misguided attempt to show the Cebuans the might of the Spanish lions ended in his death.

Throughout the journey, Pigafetta carefully wrote down details of the dress, customs, physical appearance, everyday lives, and tools of the natives. "They have boats called canoe made of one single but flattened tree, hollowed out by use of stone. Those people employ stones as we do iron, as they have no iron" he wrote about the natives of Verzin (Brazil) (page 10). He also learned to converse with the natives and kept records of their language. Today Pigafetta's journal is considered "one of the most significant documents of the Age of Discovery" (Bergreen, page 416).

Glossary

bow: the front of a ship
bowsprit: a spar that extends from the bow of the ship and supports the foremast
decks: the levels of a ship
   upper deck: the top level, extending from bow to stern
   quarterdeck: part of the upper deck, near the stern, usually reserved for officers
   poop deck: a deck that forms the roof of a cabin at the stern
   main deck: the primary level of the ship, under the upper deck
   gun deck: where the cannons were stored
   lower deck: the level just over the hold
hold: where cargo was stored
jib boom: a spar that extends from the bowsprit
masts: strong poles that hold the sails and rigging. Leo's ship had three, from bow to stern:
      foremast
      mainmast
      mizzenmast
Each mast was constructed from separate segments, from top to bottom: topgallant, topmast, lower
stern: the back of a ship
yard: a spar that runs across each mast and holds the rigging that supports the sails
yardarm: the outer part of the yard

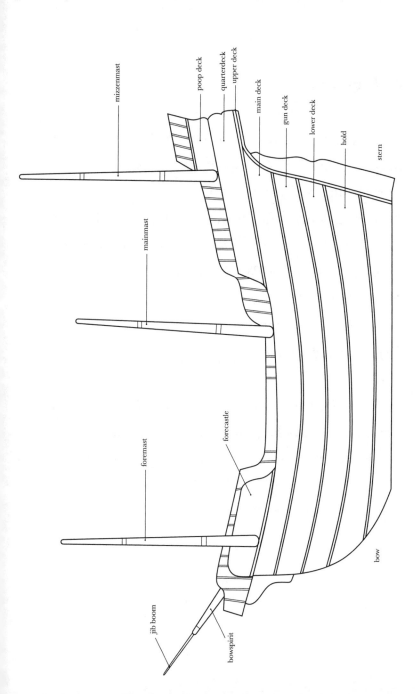

Diagram of a sixteenth-century ship

mizzenmast

poop deck

quarterdeck

upper deck

main deck

gun deck

lower deck

hold

stern

mainmast

forecastle

foremast

jib boom

bowspirit

bow

Bibliography

Bergreen, Lawrence. *Over the Edge of the World: Magellan's Terrifying Circumnavigation of the Globe.* New York: William Morrow, 2003.

Irvine, Chris. "Mary Rose's Dog Unveiled for First Time" from *The Telegraph* (*www.telegraph.co.uk/culture/culturenews/7412865/Mary-Roses-dog-unveiled-for-the-first-time.html*). March 11, 2010.

Levinson, Nancy Smiler. *Magellan: And the First Voyage around the World.* New York: Clarion Books, 2001.

Perez-Mallaina, Pablo E. *Spain's Men of the Sea.* Baltimore: John's Hopkins University Press, 1998.

Pigafetta, Antonio. *The First Voyage around the World: An Account of Magellan's Expedition.* New York: Marsilio Publishers, 1995.

For Further Reading

Bailey, Katharine. *Ferdinand Magellan: Circumnavigating the World*. New York: Crabtree Publishing Co., 2006.

Kramer, S. A. *Who was Ferdinand Magellan?* New York: Grosset & Dunlap, 2004.

Langley, Andrew. *Medieval Life*. London: Dorling Kindersley, 2011.

Levinson, Nancy Smiler. *Magellan: And the First Voyage around the World*. New York: Clarion Books, 2001.

About the Author

When Alison Hart was seven years old, she wrote, illustrated, and self-published a book called *The Wild Dog*. Since then, she's authored more than sixty books for young readers, including the *Dog Chronicles* series, *Anna's Blizzard, Emma's River,* and the *Racing to Freedom* trilogy. She lives in Virginia.

www.alisonhartbooks.com

About the Illustrator

Michael G. Montgomery creates illustrations for advertising, magazines and posters, and children's books, including the *Dog Chronicles* series, *First Dog Fala,* and *Night Rabbits*. He lives in Georgia with his family and two dogs.

www.michaelgmontgomery.com

Also in the Dog Chronicles series

Darling, Mercy Dog of World War I
HC: 978-1-56145-705-2
PB: 978-1-56145-981-0

When the British military asks families to volunteer their dogs to help the war effort, Darling is sent off to be trained as a mercy dog. She helps locate injured soldiers on the battlefield, despite gunfire, poisonous gases, and other dangers. She is skilled at her job, but surrounded by danger. Will she ever make it back home to England?

"While never shying away from the tragedies of battle, Darling's story focuses on bravery, sacrifice and devotion... Wartime adventure with plenty of heart."

—*Kirkus Reviews*

Finder, Coal Mine Dog
HC: 978-1-56145-860-8

When Thomas's family needs money, he's forced to go to work in the coal mines, even though neither of his late parents wanted that for him. His only comfort is his dog Finder, a failed hunting dog who now pulls a cart in the mines. When disaster strikes, can Thomas and Finder escape from the fires deep below ground?

"Well-told and entertaining..." —*Kirkus Reviews*

✱ NCSS / CBC Notable Social Studies Trade Books for Young People

Murphy, Gold Rush Dog
HC: 978-1-56145-769-4

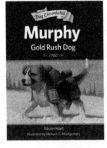

Sally and her mother have just arrived in Nome, Alaska, intent on joining the other gold seekers and making a new life there. Yet even with Murphy at their side, life in the mining town is harsh and forbidding. When it seems they may have to give up and return to Seattle, Sally and Murphy decide to strike out on their own, hoping to find gold and make a permanent home.

"Equal parts heart-wrenching and –warming… An adventure-filled tale set within a fascinating period of history." —*Kirkus Reviews*

"Readers will be quickly hooked by how Murphy tells his own story, sharing his fears, excitement, and joys." —*Booklist*